CHOKED!
Fight Until You Win

BHARATH SARMA REJETI

Cover Illustration by: Angel Dela Pena

PARTRIDGE
A Penguin Random House Company

To order additional copies of this book, contact
Partridge India
000 800 10062 62
www.partridgepublishing.com/india
orders.india@partridgepublishing.com

To the supreme power that I always believe in – God

– for giving me this ability to think, connect the dots, and weave a story for you.

And to my grandmother

– who told me the story of *The Louse and The Green Gram Dosa*, which is the inspiration for *Choked!*

Acknowledgements

I cannot but thank and seek the divine blessings of my grandmother, who told me the story of *The Louse and The Green Gram Dosa* when I was a kid. Thanks to my mother, the story has come back into my life once again when she narrated the story to my kids.

Thanks to my elder brother, Lakshmana, and my colleagues Tarak and Barada at Wipro. Their words motivated me to start on this book, and they have provided incredible inputs at various stages of the book.

Thanks to my wife, Aravinda, who assured me that the story was good when I narrated it the first time. And thanks to my friend, Jairam, who patiently heard the story and recommended a few critical changes to the plot.

I would like to thank my friends, Ravi and Nandu, who provided inputs to improve the storyline. Thanks to my close friends, Siva and Ramakrishna – they have been my pillars of strength.

Thanks to my eldest brother, Raghava, who told me the advertising war stories of Coca-Cola and Pepsi when I was young. It is because of him that I continue to perceive business competition as war and immensely enjoy day-to-day business news.

I would like to thank all my well-wishers – without their blessings, this little achievement would not have been possible.

I would also like to thank the Partridge team for bringing this book to the market.

PART I

THE CLIMAX

CHAPTER 1
THE DEAD END

Aditya Kulkarni leaped towards the wardrobe to dress quickly. He had scheduled an important appointment for that day, and he had to reach his office within two hours.

Tossing a few shirts and pushing aside a few more in the wardrobe, Aditya cried out, 'Meena, where's my dark blue tie?'

'It is right there,' Meenakshi shouted back from the dining hall.

'Where is it? I don't find it!'

Meena quickly hopped into the bedroom as if there was something in his voice that demanded her presence.

Picking up the dark blue tie from the table in front of a mirror, she stared at him, raised her eyebrows, and shook her head in disbelief. In ten years of her married life, she never understood why he always looked for things only where he expected them to be.

'I know today is an important day for you,' said Meena, tucking a hank of smooth black hair behind one ear and taming his emotions with a pleasant smile. Walking towards him and handing over the blue tie to him, she added, 'I placed this on the table so that you will find it easily.'

'Thank you.'

He smiled and stared at her briefly as she left the room. Meena was as slim as she was when he had met her the first time ten years ago. She could easily be mistaken for a newly wedded girl if she was not seen together with their two children.

Aditya was ready in another minute. Looking into the mirror, he was happy the way he looked. He was tall and lean. Except for a small little paunch that he had put on, he looked perfect, like a confident businessman, in his light blue shirt, matching trousers, and dark blue tie. Leaning towards the mirror and pushing out the upper lip with his tongue, he observed how closely he had managed to shave his moustache. Rolling over his eyes on the mirror, he then looked at his eyebrows and brushed them with his thumb. With a few specks of grey hair around his locks, his thirty-seven years of age had begun to show off.

Carrying his suit and laptop along, he reached the dining table, where he found his two kids – school-going son and daughter – and his mother waiting for him. Taking his seat and joining them, he began to have his breakfast – three *idlis* in a fine bone china plate and peanut chutney in a cup beside it.

'Hi *appa*,' greeted his son. 'Today is a big day.'

Aditya glanced at his son with a surprise and then smiled. Swallowing a small portion of an *idli* dipped in the peanut chutney, he thought, *Not bad. He knows my business schedule!*

'Sachin is going to play against the Sri Lankans! He will thrash them all and hit a century, no?' Aditya's son was visibly excited.

That was the known side of his son – always lived in the world of cricket and recognised Sachin Tendulkar as the sole member of the Indian squad.

'Hope so.'

Swallowing another portion of the *idli*, Aditya smiled and looked at his daughter and mother. Subconsciously, he also glanced at the wall clock for a quick time check. The appointment at his office was so important that he needed to rush.

'*Appa*,' said his daughter, 'our teachers are taking us on a day-picnic to Nandi Hills. I need your signature as your consent to the picnic.'

'*Amma* can sign, no?'

'*Amma* wants me to check with you first.'

Uncertain whether Aditya would agree or not, his daughter looked a little anxious. Meena gave a knowing smile from behind.

'Let *amma* sign. It's OK. I have to rush now.'

Aditya's daughter exchanged a quick happy glance with her grandma and resumed eating her *idlis* happily.

Finishing his plateful of *idlis* and a glass of orange juice, Aditya washed his hands and then glanced at the wall clock again. Meena, in the meantime, gathered a pair of clean bluish-grey socks out of a rack and held it for him.

Rushing towards the foyer and picking up the socks, he smiled and said, 'Thank you so much!'

He then said a quick prayer and bowed before his father's garlanded photograph across the hall. Just when he was about to leave, he turned back and said goodbye to his mother and kids.

'Good luck,' said his mother. Meena too wished him the best.

'Thank you.'

Aditya wished his father was alive, especially on that particular day.

His father, Uday Kulkarni, was the founder of the business he had been running over the last few years. Kulkarni Metal Products was founded in early 1980s with fasteners as the only product line. It was Uday's sharp business acumen and focused approach that had helped the business to scale up from a very small business to a reputed mid-sized business. That year, the company had clocked a little over twenty-five crores in sales.

When Aditya was a college-going kid, Uday had explained once that the fasteners product line was so chosen for the simplicity in its manufacturing process. All that Uday had to do was procure tons of steel bars in varying lengths, heat them at one end, and a stamping device would create the fastener head in a snap. The bars were then to be water-cooled, chiselled at the other end, and put through a threading lathe. In less than five minutes, the fasteners would then be ready for shipment. He minted money by producing thousands of such fasteners.

When Aditya had joined the family business, Uday taught him how important it was to procure uncompromisingly high-quality raw material and keep the process clean and simple.

Aditya had worked along with his father when he expanded the business to manufacture steel chain-pulley blocks and lever hoists that were used for heavy duty lifting and pulling. These product lines were chosen when Uday realised that his international customers in ports and shipyards lacked high quality, affordable, steel chain-pulley systems. By sticking to the same *mantra* of high quality standards, the new business lines had a phenomenal take-off. Then on, Uday never looked back. The company had a raging business.

Stepping out of the home, Aditya noticed his car driver was ready at the wheel. Sneaking into the sedan, he threw his suit and laptop in one corner of the rear seat and said, 'Make it fast. We need to reach office by 9.30 a.m.'

'OK, *saar*.'

When Kulkarni Metal Products was set up in the Whitefield Export Promotion Zone, the factory was close to Bengaluru city. Now, it is considered to be a part of the city.

From his home in Indiranagar to the factory in Whitefield, Aditya needed to cover eighteen kilometres. Ten years ago, he used to take about forty-five minutes to reach his office, but now he would take over one and half hours; especially after the International Technology Park was inaugurated in 1998 in this area, the roads towards Whitefield had never been the same. With every passing year, Aditya had witnessed more apartments developed, and a swarm of cars added to the streets at an exponential rate.

On reaching the Marathahalli flyover, a bottleneck en route to his office, Aditya glanced at his wristwatch. Traffic crawled here at snail's pace, courtesy, a never-ending flyover extension. But he felt comfortable as he still had one more hour to reach his office.

Aditya then heard his mobile phone ringing. It was Jürgen Knopfler, the director of procurement and quality assurance at United Petro, one of the biggest Oil & Gas companies in the world.

'Hi, Jürgen. Good morning.'

If it were another client, Aditya would have addressed him by the last name. He had been working with Jürgen for over eight years. Jürgen had insisted that he called him by his first name – just like his father did in the past. Jürgen had helped his business to grow by referring new clients in international ports and shipyards business.

'Very good morning, Aaditiya,' said Jürgen still struggling with that slight tongue-twisting Indian name. 'I am on my way out of the hotel. I shall reach your office shortly.'

'Sure, see you soon.' Aditya was happy that things were going as planned that morning.

Jürgen had visited the Kulkarni Metal Products factory at Whitefield earlier, but he was back in the city for a mandatory quality assessment of a new, improved, high-specification range of High Diametric Pipelines – a product line that Aditya had developed and put into production in recent years.

If Aditya could demonstrate high quality and win an order for the new high diametric pipelines, he would take the company's growth to the next level. As these pipelines are usually deployed for oil and gas distribution, the volume and scale of business would only get bigger. With the likely new order, he could build a huge *godown* for these pipelines and effectively use his 20-acre industrial plot.

Zipping through the Whitefield Export Promotion Zone, Aditya looked through the window and found numerous software company units. With every passing year, more and older manufacturing units made their way to newer, swanky software offices. Located almost at the fag-end of the Export Promotion Zone, Kulkarni Metal Products was however one of the last few surviving manufacturing companies here.

Aditya was reminded of how his father had started the business with a small 5-acre allotted industrial plot but, gradually and intelligently, acquired three more adjacent plots from his business friends. Uday ploughed back retained profits into the business and acquired land only when he needed for expansion. Following a similar strategy, Aditya had not acquired any land after his father's death. But he might need a large industrial plot if he could clinch the deal from Jürgen that day.

As he approached the factory location, Aditya noticed that the driver had considerably slowed down the car. Looking through the front windshield, Aditya saw loads of people on the street.

'What's this – some *dharna*?' It was not common to see any *dharnas* in this part of Bengaluru. What's more, Whitefield had been the quietest industrial area – thanks to the proliferation of software units.

'*Gottilla saar . . .*' In Kannada, *Gottilla* means *don't know*.

As the car crawled through the crowd, the human faces began to look increasingly familiar. These were workers from the neighbouring factory, as Aditya could recognise now. All of them had a similar puzzled expression on their faces.

Feeling restless with a likely delay, he glanced at the watch again, and felt relieved that he still had another twenty-five minutes for Jürgen to join him.

Aditya then recognised that the newer faces in the crowd were his own factory workers! And the workers looked not just puzzled but, actually, shocked!

'What's happening here?' Aditya murmured confusingly.

This time the driver did not respond as he too was lost in observing the crowd – all were known people, and they sported an inexplicable shock.

Aditya soon realised that his entire fifty-member workforce was outside the factory. His mind searched for a possible reason.

Are these guys on strike? he thought.

That could be one possibility. But this company had not witnessed a single worker strike since the inception of the business. In spite of the global slowdown in the recent months, he had neither sacked any worker nor cut their wages.

Then what was this? It was still inexplicable.

It is definitely not a worker strike, he thought. Aditya did not notice: While most of the workers looked like zombies, they performed the traditional greeting: '*Namaskara saar!*' But Aditya would not hear them until he rolled down his car windows.

Losing focus in the sea of his workers outside his car, he feebly heard a gentle knock on the other side of the windows. When he turned around, he found Kannan – lean, tall, curly haired, and sporting his trademark cylindrical spectacles. Beside him was Pratap – broad shouldered, medium built, and fair complexioned. Kannan was the finance manager, his right hand in the company, and Pratap was the manager of human resources. Their otherwise cheerful faces looked inexplicably shocked that day.

Opening the door, Aditya asked, 'What happened?'

Kannan and Pratap looked at each other glumly as if no one was sure of what had happened. Both of them were actually unsure where to start and how to say it. Aditya felt even those few seconds of silence unsettling.

Kannan grabbed Aditya's hand and pulled him like a child through the crowd towards the main gate. Reaching to the chained and locked main gates, Kannan said, 'We don't know how this has happened. I am scared and hate to say, but we seem to have lost our factory!'

'What?'

Scanning the premises inside, Aditya found a parked police van and a battalion of policemen around it. He could also find a parked police jeep beside it.

Taking Aditya to the lawyer notice that was stuck on the compound wall, Kannan said, 'Singhania did it! Please take a look at this.'

Aditya's face turned red as his eyes bulged out in shock.

'Singhania? How?'

As per the lawyer notice stuck on the compound wall, Kulkarni Metal Products' 20-acre industrial plot had pockets of *Karaab* land, something which was originally marked for weaker sections of the society. In order to regularise the plot through penalties, the company was sent several notices earlier. And subsequent to no response from the company, the civic authorities had invited public bids through an open tender. Singhania Enterprises was the winning bidder in this seemingly transparent process conducted by the authorities concerned.

'Absolutely rubbish!' screamed Aditya. 'We never received any court notices informing us about the irregularities or a need to relinquish the land, did we?' Aditya stared intensely at Kannan.

'No, we never got any such notice.'

'Then what the hell is this?' screamed Aditya.

Aditya noticed a senior policeman accompanied by a lawyer walking towards them.

'Sir, we do not want you to create any scene here,' said the senior policeman, handing over a file. 'All the relevant documents are here for your review. It will be better for you to understand the ground reality and move on.' The policeman's voice was coarse, and he said that in terse and arrestingly sharp words.

Grabbing the file, Kannan began glancing through the documents. With trembling hands, he sifted one document after another. By the time he reached the last document, he was perspiring heavily.

'Aditya, this is all very well-planned.' Kannan felt a lump building in his throat as he said these words. 'There is no way out!' He removed his spectacles and reached out to his handkerchief.

'I never imagined that crook, Singhania, would do this to us,' said Pratap.

'Can we really not fight our case?' asked Shaji Nair who had just joined them through the crowd. Shaji was the production manager at the factory.

'I really doubt it,' said Kannan.

With his legs trembling incessantly, Aditya could barely stand any longer and finally he collapsed at the factory main gate. Squatting on the ground, folding his legs, and bringing them towards him, he buried his face in his knees and began to cry.

Jürgen Knopfler reached the main gate of Kulkarni Metal Products at that time. When Pratap and Kannan briefed him on the crisis, Jürgen was speechless for a while.

'This is a daylight robbery!' exclaimed Jürgen after sometime. 'Would no one in India care for you?'

Pointing towards the policemen and the lawyer on the other side of the gate, Pratap said, 'Everyone in India seems to have a price to be bought over.'

Jürgen came face-to-face with high-level corruption and political-bureaucratic-corporate nexus that day. While he felt sorry for Aditya, he could hardly help him at that time. He enjoyed a healthy business relationship, which seemed to come to an abrupt end – an unexpected climax that Jürgen hated, but he had a business to run and therefore preferred to carry on.

Reaching to Aditya, who still had his head buried in his knees, Jürgen said, 'Aditya, I worked together with your father and you for a long time. I know how your father built this factory – brick by brick. It is very shocking and difficult to come to terms on this crisis. I will come back to India again whenever you need me and I will be glad to help you fight your case. My working relationship can be one of the legal evidences to prove your case. Just let me know when you need me. But right now, I have to leave you. I am very sorry.'

Aditya did not look up. No businessman could ever imagine sitting before a client like that – in front of his factory, on the ground, broke, broken-down with unstoppable tears!

Jürgen left the place in utter shock and disbelief.

Kannan, Pratap, and Shaji had a quick private conversation. In under a minute, Shaji and Pratap disappeared into the sea of workers. Soon after, workers began to leave the place silently. All workers had great respect for Aditya, and in a sign of empathy for him, they left the place without any noise, leaving behind only Shaji, Pratap, and Kannan.

Aditya still sat there, broken down.

What would he do now? Where would he go? He felt as if the universe no longer had any oxygen for him to breathe. He felt as if the lifeblood running in his body had suddenly vanished. His business was his daily dose of oxygen and it was his lifeblood. And somebody had snatched it away that day. He was paralysed to imagine a life without his business.

Aditya thought about only one person – his father. Uday built this factory, brick by brick, and taught him everything – to treasure the relationships at home or office. Kulkarni Metal Products was the prized legacy that he left to be protected and grown. Aditya was engulfed in a wave of sadness when he felt that his father, watching him from the heaven, would hate losing this precious little prize and the family of workers.

Aditya then remembered his mother, Meena, and his kids. How could he explain this to them? He scaled up this business to pass it on to his children one day – just like his father did. If that precious life ahead was stolen, what could he explain them?

If life were to go in a straight lane, Aditya had hit the dead end of that straight lane that day.

He needed to find a way out. Accepting a conspiracy without a fight would be as good as being part of it. And to quit without a fight this early would be like turning back on life and living the rest of the life in self-inflicted torture.

When the spirit of revolt woke up, even as he was broken down in shock, Aditya felt a sudden gush of energy – a determination to fight with Singhania.

'No. This is not fair. It is a criminal conspiracy and I will not accept this. I shall fight my case!' Aditya raised his head up after a long time. Wiping the tears off his cheeks, putting on a brave face and turning towards Kannan, he said, 'Yes, I shall fight my case. It does not matter even if it is Singhania!'

'Let's meet up with a good lawyer,' said Kannan.

CHAPTER 2
THE BIG REAL ESTATE PLAN

Vivek Mathur glanced at his BlackBerry mobile. It was 9.58 a.m. He was waiting along with his team for the chairman who was to join them in another two minutes.

He glanced across the boardroom, a large hall that appeared rich with its walls decked up in complete walnut wood, shining and partially reflecting the interiors along its flawlessly polished mirror-like surface. The room had two doors, opening into the office space on one side of the room. On the other side, the room had two large windows, overseeing the exuberant Arabian Sea. Behind the closed window blinds, the sea resonated with Vivek's mood – building each tide with excitement as it peaked at its crest and anxiously smashed as it dived into its trough. Inside the room, however, a long reddish mahogany centre table seemed perennially calm and happily smiling – it was glowing beneath the cove lighting reflected from the ceiling. The centre table was a large one, flaunting its grandeur as it spread from one end of the room to the other. The room could easily accommodate about thirty-five people, but Vivek and his six-member team sat in one section, closer to the presentation area.

Vivek then glanced at his team: it was quiet at the outset, but nervousness reflected in their behaviour. One guy tapped the table gently but restlessly, another feverishly flipped the pages of his notes as if he were a little boy cramming up at the last minute before an exam. One guy was lost in making circles over the top of circles, not knowing how many he made on the notepad in the last few minutes. Yet another guy sipped some water and gently cleared his throat for the tenth time.

All of them would have loved to avoid attending this session, but it would happen only once in a quarter. That's the time when they would come face-to-face with the chairman.

Just when the digital clock on the wall indicated 10 a.m., Gaurav Singhania, the chairman of Singhania Enterprises, walked in with a gait that carried along his confidence and reflected a strong passion for his dreams. As if his goals were constantly before his eyes, and his legs would only religiously chase them, his gait indicated a purpose and, more than all, commanded respect.

Vivek and his team rose from their seats. 'Good morning, sir!'

For anyone else, this would have appeared like a classroom of boys greeting their teacher. But this was the culture nurtured here – the one that bound Singhania's flock in a net of informal rules and restrictions. A few sarcastically relished it as *old-fashioned.*

'Very good morning, boys!'

Singhania was of average height – maybe five feet and six inches – with a clean-shaven, rounded face; he looked very fresh for the day. While he appeared a little stout, he moved with great agility. At forty-five years of age, he still had the same aggression that he had when he was much younger.

Placing his diary on the table and taking his seat in an Italian leather armchair, he said, 'Please, go ahead!'

Everyone else, in the meantime, had taken their seats.

'Sir, let me start with the good news,' said Vivek Mathur, the CEO of Singhania Realty. 'We have clinched another deal in Bengaluru. This is a sprawling 20-acre land in Whitefield. As we planned earlier, this will mark the beginning of our execution of bigger projects in the future,' added Vivek as he looked at Gaurav Singhania with pride.

Nodding his head, Singhania had a satisfactory smile on his face. With his seat pushed away from the table, he was visible in full for everyone in the room. By this time, he had his right leg folded and placed on his left knee. Moving his chin away from the neck, he held his head in a slightly inclined angle – a trademark of proud Singhania. For the rest of the team, he looked like a majestic lion in the leather armchair.

Only Singhania and Vivek in that room had the real background on how that particular deal was a *steal!*

Looking at everyone else in the room, Vivek added, 'We have decided that we will not undertake small projects here on. The days of 5-6 acre projects are well behind us. Singhania Realty henceforth will stand for mega projects.'

Turning towards Singhania, he then said, 'Sir, our operations team is lining up many other plots that are more than 20-25 acres.'

'Vivek, I need to see more action. If I don't have another two deals in the next quarter, all this will remain a mere talk.' Singhania's voice was stern. 'I need some real action in Bengaluru. It is still a very nascent market that I wish to capture in a big way.'

Singhania was probably correct in drawing his conclusions. With the headquarters and origins in oil and gas business in Mumbai, he had diversified into real estate business about eight years ago. Realising that Mumbai would ultimately be land-challenged, he had initiated this business in Bengaluru, a fast growing South Indian city. Bengaluru was a small market, but it certainly had a vast scope to spread out radially which Mumbai clearly lacked. Singhania had carefully undertaken small but several residential projects that redefined the urban lifestyle, ensuring a roaring success.

'Coming back to the just-acquired 20-acre plot, I need you guys to start the paperwork. Get all the plans and approvals needed. This has to be the most luxurious villa project ever undertaken in Bengaluru. I want the media to be talking about us very soon,' added Singhania.

'Yes sir,' responded Vivek. 'We are planning to accommodate 120 ultra-luxury villas. We have gone through some Spanish designer's collections, and we will present to you a detailed plan very shortly.'

Moving on to another agenda item for review, Singhania said, 'Great. What about the mini-township plan? Where are we on it?'

Singhania had intensified his realty plans in Bengaluru. While he had started with small residential projects, he always had plans for large commercial projects as well as townships that would elevate his corporate image in the country. He had pushed his men continuously to scale up their operations.

'Sir, our guys have been scanning the entire city and the outskirts. There are two 100-acre prospective sites that our guys are considering near the new International Airport,' answered Vivek.

'How many kilometres are they from the Hebbal flyover?' Singhania probed. He had this ability to get to the details very fast.

'About forty kilometres.'

'Too far,' said Singhania with a frown on his face. 'I don't need far-flung sites right now. I need something within the city limits to demonstrate our capability to undertake mega townships quickly. If you acquire sites forty kilometres away now, when will you start the project? Our investors cannot wait another ten years for their returns.'

Singhania had a stellar listing of Singhania Realty on the stock market the previous year. With a land bank of 250 acres and annual sales of over 450 crores, Singhania Realty was still a small realty company in the country. He wanted the company gate-crash into the top ten.

'Fine, sir. We will look for sites closer to the city,' said Vivek.

Singhania had visited Bengaluru several times in the last few years to familiarise himself with the city and to identify potential residential hotspots.

'Scan the entire stretch around the Outer Ring Road. I am sure you will find something that is not too far from it. And big enough for a township. I want nothing less than 80-100 acres.'

'Sure, sir.'

'I need to see one finalised location for a mega township by the next quarterly review!' Singhania gave his ultimatum.

'Yes, sir. We will find one.'

Looking towards the director of finance, Singhania asked, 'Do you need any disbursements and approvals now?'

Pushing forward a set of documents for Singhania's review, the director of finance said, 'Sir, we have finalised on two new project sites. One is a 2-acre plot on the Outer Ring Road near Koramangala. And another one is a 1.5-acre site near Nagarabhavi, off Mysore Road.'

After a brief pause, the director of finance continued, 'We need thirty plus twenty. That is fifty crores to proceed further on these.'

Pushing forward another set of documents for Singhania's review, Vivek said, 'We are almost finalising on three more potential sites in various parts of the city. We need an approval of twelve crores towards advances.'

Briefly flipping through the documents, Singhania summed up, 'Sixty-two crores for now?'

'Yes, sir.'

'That should be fine.' Singhania sounded comfortable with those cash disbursements and approvals. He added, 'What about the current projects – how much is available and how much is needed there?'

'For the six projects at various stages, we estimated that we would need about seventy-five crores in the next quarter.'

'Do you have loan sanctions for the same?'

'Sir, our existing working capital limits and the new sanctions that we got last week will provide access to about forty-eight crores,' said the director of finance.

'Do you want an inter-group borrowing or pledge some shares for the balance amount?'

'I believe pledging is . . .' Even before he completed his words, Singhania said 'OK' with a smile. He knew the former option would come with some strings attached and would be a little laborious. Pledging shares with their known financial institutions would be only a call away for the director of finance.

'Thank you.' The director of finance heaved a sigh of relief.

Turning his attention to the director of sales & marketing, Singhania asked, 'Satish, how are you doing on your numbers?'

'Sir, we have managed to get about twenty-seven bookings in the three just-launched projects. The other three projects are doing fine – we have completed 40 per cent bookings,' said Satish Kumar.

'But having twenty-seven bookings in the three new projects is not great. It has been over two months since they were launched. I need more,' Singhania demanded.

'Sure, sir.'

'Anything else, folks?' Singhania threw an open question as if he was ready to wrap up the meeting. The team around the table was happy that not much flak was thrown at them that day. Probably, Singhania was happy with the recently clinched 20-acre plot deal in Whitefield.

There was a brief silence in the room. Realising that the team would be glad to get dispersed, Singhania said, 'OK, folks, keep rocking. Leave me alone with Vivek for a few minutes.'

Leaving Singhania and Vivek behind, the rest of the team left the room, one by one.

Hearing the door creak and shut behind the last man, Singhania asked, 'Did that Aditya Kulkarni create any scene?'

'No, sir. He left the place without any noise.'

'Good.'

'What are you hearing though?'

'He tried meeting me at my office over the next few days. We shooed him away. No news after that. I don't think he has either approached the Press or any lawyers. But I believe he will initiate a legal case against us.'

'Vivek, I will not tolerate any legal nuisance. Bring our lawyer up to speed on the situation. Remember, nobody can dare to fight Singhania!'

CHAPTER 3
THAT SINKING FEELING

Aditya had circled Vivek's office like a hawk for almost a week. On the first day, he was told that Vivek was busy in a meeting which never ended. Every time he had checked for Vivek's availability during the day, he was told that the meeting might end any moment, but it was never started in the first place. On the second day, he was told that Vivek was out for a meeting and would be back in the office soon. But the truth was that Vivek had never stepped out for any meeting. On the third day, when Aditya found no one except the receptionist in the office, he was told that the entire team was out for an offsite workshop. On the fourth day, he thought he was finally lucky to catch hold of Vivek, when he made a surprise appearance in the lobby. But when he disappeared in a flash, the receptionist told that there was an emergency and he had to urgently catch a flight to Mumbai.

Aditya could see through all the drama, but he was angry when his honest attempt to meet and resolve the issue amicably was misconstrued as defenceless, foolish, and weak. Submissive as he was thought to be, he was not just denied an opportunity to meet Vivek but was also made to come to office every morning and wait indefinitely until the close of the day. Only after he was finally shooed away as if he was a beggar on the street, it was clear to him on how Vivek perceived him – that he neither had teeth to bite nor guts to scare.

As clear as it could be, Aditya began to see that his battle would only begin by initiating a legal action against Singhania Enterprises.

Just when he began keying in the mobile number of a reputed lawyer, Aditya noticed an incoming call on his mobile phone.

'Aditya here.'

'Mr Kulkarni,' said the caller, 'we are shocked to know that your factory has been closed for the last four days, and you had no courtesy to keep us informed.'

Aditya instantaneously recognised the caller. It was one of his US-based customers who had placed an order for a huge volume of custom-designed fasteners worth eleven crores. Moreover, his order was more or less ready for shipment. If all was well, he would have shipped the consignment by now.

'I am really sorry,' said Aditya. 'This happened all of a sudden. I am in the process of sorting out some personal issues. But I can ship . . .'

'I am sorry to inform you, but we are cancelling the order. We cannot deal with an out-of-business company.'

'I am sorry, but . . .'

The caller cut the call.

Saddled with this bad news, Aditya dropped and dissolved into the sofa in the lobby of Vivek's office. The customer who had called him was a new customer to Kulkarni Metal Products, and his custom-designed fasteners would not sell anywhere else in the world. And the size of the order was so big that the entire cash flow would get affected, potentially throwing him out of business.

Aditya was already low with the events that had unravelled in the past few days. He felt as if he was drowned in water but latched on to a supporting rope anchored to the shore – the only hope that he could begin his business. That supporting rope was now cut. Not only had he lost his land, he would now lose the business completely with this order cancellation. He began to feel that sinking feeling.

Aditya, Kannan, and Pratap had spent three days running around and seeking an important legal appointment and finally managed to get it one day. They patiently waited for their turn, for all the reputation that this lawyer had in the city. As each of the prior appointments spilled over, they waited in the hall for over three hours.

The trio now sat across the table in Rahul Gonsalves's office as he scrutinised the documents.

Peering through his reading lenses and narrowing his eyes in fierce concentration, Rahul took a considerably long time to read each page.

Aditya began to observe the room in the meanwhile. Behind Rahul's seat, an enormous bookshelf, made in fine teak, looked like a walk-in legal library. The shelf had numerous thick-volume books that appeared uniformly in their brick-red-coloured spines and gold-coloured alphabets.

Meanwhile, Rahul found a set of documents related to Aditya's land and associated sale deeds. A few surveys within the large piece of land indicated that it had parcels of government-owned land which was earmarked for weaker sections of the society. The file had a few copies of letters issued out to Kulkarni Metal Products, primarily bringing the existing irregularities to their notice and demanding some penalty. It also had photographs of lawyer notice stuck on the compound wall – photographs were dated with printed dates on them. The dates on the photographs and those of the letters were close enough. One could easily back date a camera setting, but it would be difficult to contest what had come from a government body.

Rahul then found a set of newspaper advertisements – those from *Karnataka-Suddi, Bengaluru-Sanje* and *The City Times*. All these newspapers had one of the lowest circulations in the city but enough to attract government tender advertisements. So Rahul inferred that he would not be able to challenge the chosen media. The first set of advertisements was notices of expropriation of Aditya's property in Whitefield and the other set was related to invitation of open tenders to bid for government-expropriated property. Finally, the file had documents related to the bids received and transactions the government had with Singhania Realty.

Singhania had managed to win the bid for the 20-acre plot for just ten crores!

A few minutes ago, Rahul had also scrutinised the original land documents that Aditya provided, and they all had a different story to tell.

Rahul pushed his reading spectacles into his thick, bushy white hair. It was clear that he finished with his scrutiny of the documents.

Closing the file in hand, Rahul closed his eyes for a minute and massaged the nose where his spectacles rested so far. Gently throwing the file on to the table, he then shook his head in disbelief.

'What's your take, sir?' asked Aditya eagerly.

Rahul opened his eyes and looked at Aditya.

Aditya looked very pale. He had grown a little jawline beard and moustache. It was clear that the shocking incident had a tremendous effect on him. He skipped his daily shaving routine, and it looked as if he had not even looked himself in the mirror for the last seven days. With his hair uncombed and his eyes blood red, it was palpable that Aditya had slept very little too.

'No . . . ,' said Rahul, dragging the word uncomfortably long. He then shook his head in disbelief, again.

Aditya stared at him as if he was not satisfied with a short answer. His eyes still probed Rahul to add something more.

'This is a meticulous job,' inferred Rahul. 'They have evidence for anything and everything that I can think of.'

Pointing to another file on the table, Aditya asked, 'What about these originals?'

'What about them?' asked Rahul sternly and stared at Aditya's face. 'You can only say, look here, this is my land. But Singhania has evidence that there were irregularities, notices for penalties, notices of expropriation, invitation for open tenders in local newspapers, and all transactional documentation to support his case!'

'But you know that they are all fake!'

'Yes, I know. But that does not help me to win you the case.'

Aditya was stunned. He looked quizzically as he stared at Rahul.

'I don't think I can create enough counter-evidences to fight your case,' concluded Rahul uncomfortably. 'I am absolutely sorry.'

Aditya lost all his courage at once. He had come here with a lot of hope that Rahul would certainly help him. *With the most renowned and fearless lawyer in the city backing out, who else can help me?* he thought.

Leaning his head forward, Aditya faced the wooden table that he was seated across. Slowly and gradually, he leaned forward until his forehead hit the tabletop in despair.

Feeling the dejection that Aditya was undergoing, Pratap asked, 'Mr Gonsalves, we have come to you with great hopes. Your reputation of being fearless and fair has brought us here. I hope you understand that our case is genuine. If someone can think and create fake evidences to throw us out of our business, I am sure you can take up the case and help us legally fight our case.'

'I wish I could,' answered Rahul and then added, 'I certainly understand that you are a genuine party. But legally speaking, I am helpless with this level of sophistication of evidences that the other party already has.'

Pratap did not know what to say and convince him. Kannan was also speechless.

The room was engulfed in a long silence. Aditya managed to lift his head up, staring into infinity. He had no more tears left to cry. He had cried enough and cursed himself several times in the last few days. But the look on his face indicated that he was emotionally and visibly broken now.

He had cursed himself because this was not his first encounter with Singhania.

Starting from early last year, Singhania's men had approached Aditya for a potential outright sale of his factory with all its assets. He had politely refused the offer and asked them to leave him with the only business that he had been running. When the field-level men were sent back without a deal, Singhania had sent a manager, who offered to buy the property for 100 crores. By no means, it was a fair deal. Aditya had to reject the offer again – that time he clearly mentioned that he had kids, whose future he needed to secure. And his business was the only future that he had been building for them. Indeed, all he ever had besides his home was his factory.

But Singhania had relentlessly sent his men. Manager after manager, many had visited him at his factory and hiked the offers. At the last instance, Aditya was offered 200 crores, which was far lower than the market rate. If one were to consider his business which was worth twenty-five crores in sales, the plant and machinery, his inventory and the current assets, and with absolutely no debt on the balance sheet, a fair deal would have been 450 crores to buy out the entire business.

He cursed himself not for leaving a lucrative financial offer that he had received earlier, but for the promises that he had made to his father on the deathbed – that he would take care of the business and his family. Aditya was too emotionally attached to something that his father had built.

Even in his wildest dreams, Aditya had never expected Singhania would grab his land against his wishes. It was indeed a steal for Singhania – ten crores for a 20-acre plot!

Realising that dredging the past and self-inflicting more pain would be futile, Aditya regained his senses. 'Fine then,' said Aditya. His voice was completely choked. Clearing his throat, he rose from his seat and added, 'Thank you for your time and opinion on this case, Mr Gonsalves.'

'What did the lawyer say?' asked Meena curiously when Aditya returned home.

'He said that he cannot fight our case.'

'Why?'

'He feels that Singhania has every proof needed to win the case.'

Meena paused for a while and then said, 'If he feels so, so be it. But I feel that we can find someone else who can fight and win our case.'

'He is the best in the city!'

'I don't care,' said Meena. 'God will show us someone else who is worthwhile.'

Meena was also his philosopher and best friend. Her words usually worked a magic on him.

'I really hope so,' said Aditya. 'I am doing my bit – searching for another lawyer.'

Over the next four days, Aditya visited several lawyers in Bengaluru. None of them were ready to take up his case. Some had shared a similar opinion to what Rahul Gonsalves had. The rest had expressed a fear for their life if they had to choose fighting a case against Singhania.

Singhania Enterprises and its listed group companies were one of the most actively traded stocks in the market. Just the size of the group, at 9,500 crores, could instil fear in fighting a case against Singhania. Fear, as it appeared to Aditya, could consume human mind faster than reality. Fear had completely eclipsed the facts that could be gathered to fight the case.

With every rejection, however, Aditya began to feel more dejected. With every rejection, he felt less motivated to approach new lawyers. With every rejection, a new door of an opportunity to fight his case was closed. With every rejection, he moved much closer to the dead end of his life.

Aditya began to appear scruffy. He had unshaven beard and undressed hair for the entire week. His skin got burnt in sun, and his care in choosing the attire had considerably diminished. If he was not seen together with Kannan and Pratap on all these lawyer visits, he would have been unattended or mistaken for a shabby beggar on the roadside.

By that weekend, Aditya was clear that Bengaluru had no lawyer willing to fight his case. Physically exhausted, mentally tired, and completely fatigued, Aditya saw no visible road that he could explore.

Is this the end of my life? he questioned one more time.

At home, his kids were increasingly concerned. The mandatory family breakfast was done without Aditya, and the kids were unaware of the entire story. They only noticed that

Aditya had stopped going to the factory but did not know exactly why.

In the meantime, with increasing number of rejections, Meena had begun to fear for his life. Until he returned home late in the evening each day, her mind unwantedly explored fearful thoughts. While Meena cried a number of times when her children were away at school, she had managed to put on a brave face while they were around at home. But she continued her prayers and believed in a miracle that God alone could make it happen.

'Any luck?' asked Meena that evening.

Aditya just shook his head in denial.

Putting on a brave face and patting his back, Meena said, 'Don't worry. Truth shall win. If not today, some other day. Wrongdoers will be punished, and we have nothing to fear.'

Aditya did not speak a word. He wished that Meena was right with those words – something his brain needed to gather some strength.

———◆◇◆———

At about 11 p.m. that night, Aditya opened his Facebook page. It had two notifications – private messages – one from Jürgen, his client contact at United Petro, and another from Prof. Srinivas, an independent director and board member at Kulkarni Metal Products.

Jürgen's private message said, 'It was very disturbing to see you in such a state the other day. I hate to say this, but please don't do anything stupid . . . Did you initiate any legal case? Just ping me for any help that you might need. Please keep me posted.'

Aditya reread the part that said: 'I hate to say this, but please don't do anything stupid . . .'

He knew what Jürgen was thinking about.

Over the week, Aditya felt very dejected. Luckily, he still had not lost all hope. While the lawyers closed their doors, he now wanted to meet Singhania directly and sort out the issue.

Aditya felt that nobody could take his business away from him. *Nobody can ever do that*, he thought.

What's more, he camped again at Vivek's office that morning, and Vivek had given into his pressure. When Vivek explained that there was nothing much he could do, Aditya tried calling up Singhania's Mumbai office to schedule a meeting. He still had no luck in reaching Singhania, though.

'I might have lost my land but not my hope . . . I will be meeting Singhania shortly to sort this out. Thank you for dropping this message. I will keep you posted on further developments,' replied Aditya to Jürgen.

The next message from Prof. Srinivas said, 'Your phone was unreachable . . . I came to know about what has happened to you. It is simply unbelievable. Let's initiate a legal case!' The message was already eight days old.

Prof. Srinivas was on the company's board for many years. Aditya had always wanted good and reputed people on his board. An IIT-educated person and a professor at the same college, Prof. Srinivas was a brilliant engineer. His inputs on mechanical engineering had redefined productivity at Kulkarni Metal Products. Settled in Chennai, he visited Bengaluru for all board meetings and whenever else his expertise was needed.

Aditya replied to Prof. Srinivas's message, 'The lawyers here are timid. No one has agreed to fight our case. I am scheduling a meeting with Singhania to sort this out. Btw, my apologies: I should have informed you earlier . . .'

Over the next three days, Aditya camped at Vivek's office. He made no big noise, but Vivek was visibly frustrated. As if he set an hourly reminder, Aditya ensured that he made a call to Singhania's office every hour, throughout the day. Singhania's secretary neither put him through nor confirmed any appointment.

Finally, after two more days, he received a call. 'Mr Singhania has agreed to meet you tomorrow. 10 a.m. sharp!' The lady over the phone was brief and indifferent; she neither cared if Aditya got the message clearly nor waited for his response as an acknowledgement.

CHAPTER 4
CHOKED!

Aditya sat in the lobby of Singhania's Mumbai corporate office which looked nothing less than a five-star hotel. The contemporary architectural theme was clear in the chosen material: stone, steel, and glass. The flooring had glass-like, rich Italian marble that reflected numerous spotlights affixed to the ceiling. The sponge-finished walls had an aesthetic mix of decorative paints and matte-finished volcanic stones that blended together as an artwork. The stainless steel and glass, used in right proportions and in the right places of the lobby, reflected the richness in ambient lighting.

Aditya stared at the wall clock. It was 9.45 a.m. He still had another fifteen minutes to meet Singhania.

He is unlikely to call me at sharp 10 a.m., he thought. He managed to get this appointment after relentlessly chasing Singhania's secretary and pressurising Vivek at Bengaluru for over one week. It implied that Singhania would make him wait for a long time that day.

Aditya's blood boiled from inside since the day he had lost his property. But he repeated a number of times in his mind that he would need to retain his cool, negotiate with Singhania, and win his business back that day.

'Mr Kulkarni,' called the receptionist. Pointing towards the escalator area at the other end of the lobby, she added, 'Mr Singhania would like to see you in his office now. Please take the escalator to the fourth floor.'

'Thank you.'

Aditya glanced at the wall clock again. It was 9.55 a.m. Five minutes ahead of schedule. He could not believe his eyes.

On the fourth floor, the escalator opened directly into Singhania's office which had a mini lobby and another lady seated in one corner. As soon as he entered this floor, a hint of fresh citrus fragrance hit him in the face. The room fragrance was refreshing, but he was in no mood to rejoice in it.

'Mr Kulkarni?' said the lady.

'Yes?'

Pointing to the sofa in this room, she very politely added, 'Please wait here, sir. I shall let you know when Mr Singhania is ready.'

At 10 a.m. sharp, opening a large walnut door, the lady said, 'Sir, please . . .' The door had numerous square-shaped small mirrors stuck on it that reflected the ceiling lights, giving it a rich look and feel.

Entering the room, Aditya noticed that the office looked like a presidential suite in a five-star hotel. Singhania sat in a leather armchair, far away from the entrance, in one corner. In another corner was a large seating area, with a huge fifty-six-inch flat screen TV, running CNBC-TV18 in mute. The running ticker indicated the current market prices of the stock-market-listed companies.

Seeing Singhania walking towards the seating area, Aditya too moved towards him.

'So you are Aditya Kulkarni!' Giving a quick, firm handshake, Singhania put on a welcome smile. Giving the scrolling ticker a quick, last glance, he switched off the TV in the seating area.

Aditya said, 'Hi.'

Singhania noted that he added no suffice like 'sir'. He had been so used to everyone calling him 'sir'.

Singhania inferred that either Aditya had no manners or he was ignorant of the size of his business empire.

Singhania Enterprises was a 9,500 crores corporate gorilla with three business lines – oil and gas exploration and refining, power generation and nuclear power systems, and residential real estate. Oil and gas had contributed roughly 6,300 crores the previous year, power business some 2,750 crores, and real estate business some 450 crores.

'I thought I will see you in my office much earlier. You are one difficult man to meet,' said Singhania, taking a seat in the seating area. As he spoke, he gestured that Aditya should also take a seat.

'I should say that. I found it difficult in reaching you over the last one week and taking this appointment.'

'You are referring to the waiting you had to do for the last one week. I am referring to the waiting that I had to do for the majority of the last year. My boys were chasing you then, weren't they?' For the first time, Singhania had opened his attack directly that morning.

Aditya realised that this discussion was not going to be an easier one. He reminded himself again that he had no reason to escalate the tone of the discussion but to win his business back.

'I had no reason to take your appointment at that time. I wanted to focus on my business. I had no intention to sell it in any case.'

'What do you do, Aditya?' Singhania threw a very different question, something that Aditya had not expected.

'Sorry?'

'What was your business?'

Aditya recorded that Singhania referred to his business as if it was closed.

'I have a business of manufacturing fasteners, chain-pulley blocks, and high-diametric pipelines.' Aditya maintained that he still had the claim on his business.

'You *had* that business but not now,' said Singhania provocatively. 'But what was that you manufactured – fasteners? How big was your nut-and-bolts business?'

Aditya was clearly taken aback by Singhania's sarcastic reference to fasteners as nuts-and-bolts and more so at his claim that the business was closed.

Looking straight into Singhania's eyes, Aditya sternly said, 'It is not just nuts and bolts. I also have chain-pulley systems and pipelines. Twenty-five crores worth business.'

'Ah, twenty-five crores. Big deal! Why do you need such a big piece of land to make pittance,' said Singhania, throwing his hands up in the air. This time, Aditya found his gestures more provocative than his words.

'And for those stupid products, you were not ready to let go your e-m-p-i-r-e of twenty-five crores, ah?' Singhania turned nastier with every second sentence he uttered that morning.

Aditya's blood began to boil again.

'These are not stupid products. I have a lot of respect for what I do. Moreover, twenty-five crores is good, enough money for me and my fifty employees.' Aditya struggled to maintain his cool.

'Fine, how does it matter when you have a huge cancelled order from your US customer? Your business was officially closed!'

Aditya could not believe his ears. He heard Singhania talk about an order cancellation, which Aditya and his colleagues alone knew about. He was completely confused as to how Singhania knew about it.

'What did you say?' asked Aditya with a frustrating frown on his face.

Singhania shrugged his shoulders, raised his head, and, holding it in a patently slanting position, gave a sarcastic smile. Aditya was shocked and angry, but it was clear that Singhania had orchestrated that order cancellation to keep him out of his business.

After that US order cancellation, the entire cash flow in the business was frozen. His bankers had revoked the bank guarantee, and he was officially out of business! It was shocking for Aditya that Singhania had orchestrated this nasty episode.

'Why are you doing this to me?' asked Aditya.

Steering the conversation to a different topic again, Singhania asked, 'Did you say you manufactured high-diametric pipelines?'

'Yes, I do.'

'How come I have never heard of you?'

Aditya understood that Singhania was referring to his oil and gas business which would have been a customer for these high-diametric pipelines in distributing oil and gas.

'We have been a 100 per cent export-oriented unit right from the inception.'

Taking another chance to provoke, Singhania said, 'Oh, 100 per cent e-x-p-o-r-t-s? No wonder you have no respect for a domestic client like me!'

'I have respect for everyone. You need to ask if you have respect for me and my beliefs.'

'It is always give-and-take, my friend! You never gave me what I deserve . . . Singhania cannot be denied an opportunity, and you have done that!'

Aditya could see venom in his eyes. It was enough provocation, and Aditya began to lose his cool.

'For me, it was never about you, Mr Singhania,' said Aditya, referring him by his name for the first time that day. 'It was always about me and my family.'

Singhania did not say anything.

Realising that he had successfully managed to get his attention, Aditya added, 'This business was founded by my father. Moments before his death, I made him a promise that I will protect it, run it, and make it a better business for my children. My effort in making the business larger is the way I secure my kids' future. I have absolutely nothing else to do in my life. I politely requested your folks to let me focus on what I chose to do. You tell me what was wrong in rejecting your offers when I was not even willing to sell! I respect what you have to do in your life.'

As if his words were boring, Singhania shrugged his shoulders and said, 'Fundamentally, the problem is that you have too good a property for me to leave. And when I made an offer, you were better off to take it and vanish. And I had made not just one offer but three offers to you! I have never made a second offer to anyone else!'

'Two hundred crores was not the right price for my property. I have a twenty-five-crores-worth business running on it, which was never meant for sale!'

'Now I know why you are a lousy businessman!' Singhania threw another provocative inference.

Taken aback again, Aditya just stared at him.

'To me, a good businessman is always open-minded. You are lousy. If you were not happy with 200 crores, you should have quoted your figure and walked away with it,' Singhania said as if he was very generous at heart.

'You are missing the point, Mr Singhania. My property and my business are all that I have for this life.'

'That is no longer your property. And your business is gone for good!'

Aditya faced the harshest words. From the day he had lost the property, Aditya had been saying only one thing to himself: he would win back his business. His life was meaningless without it.

'You cannot take away my life like this.'

'You automatically lost your life when you said *no* to me!'

'You cannot do this to me. I am in ruins. I have a family to take care of. I have a promise to keep.' Aditya made a desperate plea.

'You dug your own grave. It is too late for you to visit me now. You should have come to me long ago, when I made the first offer.'

'I am sorry, but please . . . I need my life back! I have nowhere to go now!' Aditya was choked when he said this.

Turning around and throwing his hands in the air, Singhania shouted, 'Don't ask your property back. It is impossible to return it. Don't you have another property elsewhere to carry on your stupid business?'

'No. I have absolutely nothing else!' screamed Aditya.

After those loud words fell apart, there was long pause followed by pin-drop silence in the room. Singhania walked up and back to his desk a couple of times, with no hint of what was going on in his mind. But his body language and facial expressions indicated that he was thinking something intensely. He felt as if his desperate plea worked a magic, and Singhania would return his property.

Before confirming this appointment with Aditya that day, Singhania had done his homework. His lawyer's word was spread across Bengaluru. Subsequently, he had information that Aditya was denied every chance to pick up the fight legally. Vivek had updated him about his camping at the Bengaluru office and pressurising him to resolve the issue. He knew that

Aditya had no other option but to resign from everything else at this time.

Singhania glanced once again at Aditya, a tall, frail structure that was physically less demanding, in general and psychologically shaken now, in particular. Singhania had come across far too many small entrepreneurs who had a peculiar problem of buying too many small pieces of land all over the place. But Aditya genuinely appeared to have nothing else to leverage.

Singhania thought his guys had probably got a wrong guy with the right property for his ultra-luxury villa project in Bengaluru. Anyway, while Singhania would never recall his decisions, he felt he would have to do something for Aditya.

Singhania scribbled something at his desk and came back to the seating area.

Offering a cheque, Singhania provokingly said, 'I come from a very good family. I was never trained to leave a beggar empty-handed. That's fifteen crores for you – almost your annual turnover. Take it or leave it.'

'And my property? My business?' asked Aditya naively.

'You lost them, my friend. Never ever come in my way! No one can come in my way.'

Aditya stared at the cheque on the centre table.

Fifteen crores!

Aditya realised that Singhania would not budge more and give his business back. He never realised that he had rubbed Singhania the wrong way, even though he politely rejected his offers in the past.

That day's encounter with Singhania was an eye-opener for him. He realised what little respect Singhania had for small business owners like him. He had no qualms in the crime that he had done. If not arrogance, what else would make him pay fifteen crores for what easily could have fetched 450 crores!

Aditya realised that Singhania had an ego which seemed to weigh in tons. Singhania could not be won on any humanitarian grounds, for which he had come prepared with. Singhania showed no emotions, so there was no point in being sentimental about his father's property.

Aditya glanced at Singhania again. Singhania was the most materialistic businessman personified in front of him.

Aditya realised that for Singhania, he was yet another guy to be bought over, yet another guy to be silenced by his crime. Singhania had bought over people at the municipality and the police station, and he had made them his partners-in-crime. Singhania now wanted Aditya to take the leftovers.

Aditya had come with no intention to beg for his property. He wanted the only life he had known all these years. He wanted what he was carefully building for his children. But Singhania made him a beggar, throwing what he could afford to lose, a miserly sum to shut him up.

Who is he to take away what belonged to me? Aditya was breathing fire as that thought hit him. In a country where power is measured not in making money righteously but in grabbing what does not belong to them and getting away with it, his anger was pointless. The fear of hitting the dead end of his life and staring into the darkness of the future was more overwhelming than his anger. He could also sense a growing frustration that he was all alone, helpless, and left with a choice to quit or fight back. In a tsunami of emotions that engulfed him, Aditya felt completely choked!

Yes, I shall take this, Aditya said to himself after staring at the cheque for several minutes.

To plot Singhania's downfall and to bring down the empire that he was proud of – in ways that Singhania would not even have dreamt of.

Yes, I shall take this, Aditya said to himself.

To make Singhania realise of what a small fasteners guy could do, to strip him off his arrogance that he flaunted, and to rip him off all the vanity that he carried.

Yes, I shall take this, Aditya said to himself.

Not because he already knew how to strike a corporate gorilla like Singhania but because he was confident of his capability in attacking him; choking Singhania was the single objective in his life.

Still staring at the cheque of fifteen crores, Aditya wondered if he could bargain and increase the sum to plot Singhania's downfall. After a long silence in the room, Aditya finally looked back at Singhania and asked, 'But just fifteen crores for what could have been 450 crores?'

Singhania looked straight into his eyes and said, 'My place. My price. Take it or leave it!' He then just walked away to his seat at the other end of the room.

As Aditya walked out of his palatial cabin, Singhania said, 'What a loser!'

PART II

THE BEGINNING

CHAPTER 5
THE TURNING POINT

Cutting through tall, wild grass and filling the air with the sound of crushed leaf litter under his feet, Aditya moved forward in what looked like a jungle. Far aside the pathway, he found lifeless trees, baked by sun and flanked by large boulders. Aditya picked up pace as a sense of ambiguity and fear, and of why and where he had arrived, rushed up to his brain. Sweating and panting, he stepped out of thick bushes that surrounded him along the pathway. Halting his brisk footwork, he gathered a panoramic view of where he had arrived. It was a hilltop, with an incredible but a scary view of the valley below. At this height, the wind was blaring over his head – so strong that the wind pushed him gently into the bushes from where he had just come. He had never seen a place like this before – wild, windy, and intriguing.

He wanted to show Meena and his kids how wild the hilltop looked.

Where are they? he thought.

Turning around to head back and find his family, he found a giant figure emerge out of the bushes. He was very tall – maybe over seven foot in height, broad-shouldered, and dark; his naked upper body showed off painfully crafted muscles and six-pack abs. In contrast with the huge size of his body, he had a small head with closely cut hair.

Aditya stopped and stared at this intriguingly arresting giant personality.

Showing a crooked set of dark-coloured teeth, the alien smiled at him.

'Who are you?' asked Aditya.

He remained silent, still grinning and showing off his crooked teeth.

'Who are you?' demanded Aditya.

In response, this time, the giant figure pounced on Aditya and pushed him. In a single push, Aditya reached the edge of the hilltop.

Gathering himself and standing again on his feet, Aditya looked back at the giant personality in a daze.

What on earth is he doing? Aditya thought.

'What's wrong with you? What you do want?' asked Aditya.

The giant personality flexed his muscles as he intensely stared back at Aditya. His eyes turned red and large in an incomprehensive anger, and the teeth grew uncannily out of his mouth – something that gave goosebumps to Aditya instantaneously.

Is this guy a man or a monster? Aditya thought as he stared at the dark, giant person.

The exchange of intense views seemed too long, when, in comparison, the giant person began to move and reach Aditya in split seconds. Even before Aditya could judge of what the dark giant was doing, Aditya realised that he was already off the cliff. The giant person had pushed him one more time and grinned happily, flaunting his crooked teeth as Aditya began to fall into what looked like a bottomless valley.

Facing sky up, Aditya began to accelerate his fall into the wild, steep valley below. His eyes bulged out and began to look for people he wanted to see, but no one was in sight. His hands grappled to feel something, but all that he could sense was volumes of air, and it was pushing him from behind. He wanted to hear Meena and his kids one last time, but all his ears could hear was a monster roar of the wind. He knew a fall from those heights would have his head smash against the hard, rocky ground. Falling like a stone from the hilltop, Aditya felt that his spine could no longer support him and that his body might split even before he crash-landed on the ground. Gathering all the strength from within, Aditya tried one last time to turn over and face the abyss below – a physically strenuous task it was, and it sent a jolt across his body.

Aditya woke up from his sleep with a jolt on the bed!

He had neither a wild valley below nor a clear sky above. It was a nightmare.

Panting and feel exhausted, he closed his eyes and rubbed them. He never had such a bad dream in his life.

Opening his eyes and checking the time on his mobile phone, he realised that it was 11.30 p.m – not even an hour since he had slipped into a deep sleep.

Stepping out of the bed and reaching out to a bottle of cold water in the refrigerator, he felt his whole body aching with pain. He coughed as he walked towards the living room and sat on the sofa beside a window that had been left open. Filling the silence of the room, the wind came whistling through the window. Aditya shut the window to feel the silence, the only comforting sound that he wanted to hear after he had such a bad dream.

Stretching on the sofa, he stared at the ceiling, visualising hazy images of unseen future for several minutes until he finally heard someone else in the room.

It was his daughter. She squinted her eyes as she woke up and stepped out of her dark bedroom into the glare of brightly lit living room.

'*Appa*, I am unable to sleep. Can you please read a story for me?'

He wanted to dismiss her and stay alone for some more time. But he did not want to disappoint her. It was well over many days since Aditya had read a story to her.

Getting up from the sofa, he said, 'Fine.' He coughed as he walked towards her.

Switching on the bedside lamp in her room, Aditya began to read out a *Panchatantra* story as his daughter blinked her sleepy eyes.

'The story of the merchant and his iron,' Aditya read aloud from the book. 'Once upon a time in a village called Mahilaropya, there was a merchant who traded in iron. One day, he decided to leave for a faraway prosperous city in order to make more money. He then approached his friend and requested him to safeguard all the iron he had until he returned to the village.'

His daughter's droopy eyelids closed for more time than she had managed them to keep them open.

Aditya coughed again and continued to read, 'The merchant's friend assured him that he would take care of it. The merchant left the village, but he did not return for many years. Thinking that the merchant might not return, his friend sold all the iron, paid off his debts, and lavishly spent the rest of the money. But one day the merchant returned and asked for his iron. His friend cooked up a story and said that the iron was eaten by a few rats.'

Meanwhile, his daughter fell asleep.

But a curious Aditya continued to read: 'Knowing that his friend was just fooling around, the merchant decided to teach him a lesson. One day, the merchant locked up his friend's son at his home. After two days, he informed his anxious friend that he saw a sparrowhawk carrying away a boy. And the boy looked like his son! His friend asked how a small sparrowhawk could carry such a big boy. The merchant replied anything would be possible in a village in which rats could eat iron. Realising his mistake, the friend returned the merchant's money in exchange for his son!'

By the time Aditya had finished reading the story, his daughter was fast asleep. There was no point in telling her the moral of the story, he realised.

He made an inference which answered his dilemma. *The means to fight and win a war against a wilful wicked person is immaterial.*

Kannan, Pratap, and Shaji gathered in the living room of Aditya's home the next morning. Aditya had called them for an urgent meeting.

Aditya said, 'I have very bad news.' He looked very dejected after he returned from his meeting with Singhania. He wore a sweater and folded his hands closer to keep himself warm.

Coughing intermittently, he added, 'We lost our business. We lost the entire property. That crook Singhania threw away these fifteen crores.' He placed the cheque on the centre table in the living room.

The other three in the room looked at each other.

This outcome was not very different to what Singhania was reputed for. At least, Kannan was not so hopeful that Singhania would return the property. He was familiar with this real estate business and the lure of land for its suitors.

Breaking a long silence in the room, Kannan said, 'I don't know what to say.'

Recollecting his discussion at Mumbai, Aditya said, 'Singhania is a rock. He has no emotions. He threw his ego all over. He was unprepared to accept his mistake. In fact, he felt it was my mistake to reject his earlier offers.'

'He is known to be a very egoistic businessman. Even in his dreams, he will never accept his mistake,' said Kannan.

'And guess what, he orchestrated that order cancellation. When none other than the four of us know about it, Singhania brought this up in the conversation to my shock. It was he who put us out of our business!'

'Shocking!' said Kannan.

'What's your plan now?' asked Pratap curiously after a long pause.

Trying to hide the pain, Aditya said, 'I have no plan. That's what I wish to discuss with you today. I am sorry that I was unable to win back our business. I feel very sorry for what I have put you and your families through the past few weeks.'

'We are more worried about you than our business. We are all together for you to undertake anything that you plan,' said Pratap.

'I don't know what I am going to do now.' Aditya's voice choked a little as he said those words. Briefly looking up towards the ceiling, clearing his throat, and regaining his composure, he added, 'I wish to pay at least you and other employees. Pratap and Shaji, please convey to the entire shop floor workers that they will get three months of advance pay. I am sorry, I cannot do anything more.'

Shaji said, 'Sir, I never thought I will discuss these things with you. I have been in touch with every worker. Each one of them is praying for you. All of us love working with you. Let's not discuss any advance pay now. We can all pool in money and start a small venture, as you may wish.'

'I don't think that's realistic. I don't have any plan. I don't wish to put our employees in more trouble.' A visibly ill Aditya coughed intermittently.

'But, sir . . .'

Cutting Shaji short, Aditya added, 'Please. I need some time to think for myself. It is much better for you to take the advance pay and move on.'

Realising what Aditya had in mind, Pratap said, 'Fine then. We will settle the shop floor workers' pay. But I am not going to take anything.'

Kannan and Shaji joined him, saying, 'Yes, we don't need any advance pay. At least, we will wait for your next move and join you.'

'Thank you for your solidarity. If ever I have something to do, it would be just one plan.' Pausing for a moment again, he then added, 'I wish to crumble Singhania's empire to the ground.' As he said those words, Aditya looked like a tiger waiting patiently for a kill: focused, determined, and hungry.

'Tell me how I can help you. I am game for this,' responded Kannan fiercely.

'I don't know. But I shall plot his downfall for sure!' Aditya's eyes looked intense. Regaining his cool again, he added, 'I don't think you guys should be waiting for me. I am glad that you are eager to support me. I will let you know when I need your help. But right now, your families need you more than anyone else. Please consider a good job offer and move on.'

Over the next two days, Aditya settled all his shop floor workers' salary out of the money that he had managed to get from Singhania. The outgo to settle this commitment was a little over twelve lakhs. As previously pledged, his top three managers – Kannan, Pratap, and Shaji – had sacrificed their salary settlements. They all wanted the balance money to be used for Aditya's home needs. But Aditya was keen to use that money in bringing down the empire that Singhania had built.

Aditya's sleepless nights and odd eating hours had taken a toll on his health. He had fallen ill with flu, cough, and fever. One particular day, he was feeling terrible.

'Come, let's go to the hospital,' said Meena.

'No, I am fine.'

'No, you are not fine. It's been three weeks since you had some proper food. You don't sleep, you don't eat, and if at all you eat, you eat at odd hours – you cannot ignore your health, fall sick like this, and still think that you are doing fine.'

'No, I am really fine,' said Aditya, coughing ironically.

'I cannot see you like this. Wait, I am going to call the driver,' said Meena restlessly.

Recollecting that he had settled the salary of his driver too, he said, 'Why call the driver? I can go on my own.'

'I will come along,' said Meena, approaching him.

Hugging her briefly, he said, 'It's OK. I will manage.'

He did not drive his car for many years now. He was used to the comforts of the rear seat while he was driven. But in the last few days, he had begun to keep his expenses to a minimum – walking across the street to do petty shopping, talking less on phone, and other simple but smart ways to spend less.

That day, Meena pushed him to hire an autorickshaw, which he had not hired for the past many years.

'Auto?' called Aditya.

Bringing an autorickshaw to a screeching halt, one autorickshaw driver answered, '*Saar?*'

Trying to sneak into the just-halted autorickshaw, Aditya said, 'Chinmaya Hospital?'

'Fifty rupees, *saar.*'

'Fifty?!' Aditya immediately hopped out of the autorickshaw. Chinmaya Hospital was less than two kilometres from his home. It would not cost more than fourteen rupees to reach the destination.

'*Havdu, suar.* Petrol *jaasti aayathu!*' (Yes, sir. The petrol prices have increased.)

'No fifty-rupees business here! Please put on the metre,' demanded Aditya.

'*Illa, saar. Bidi.*' (No, sir. Leave it.) The auto guy zipped away immediately without even looking at him. Aditya was shocked by the auto guy's rudeness.

'Auto?' Aditya tried to hire another autorickshaw.

'Chinmaya Hospital?'

'Fifty rupees.' Different guy, but he too quoted the same rate.

Aditya then tried with three more auto guys. All had the same rate to quote – fifty rupees.

Realising that there was a cartel of auto guys, he finally negotiated a to-and-fro trip for seventy rupees. Aditya was totally unhappy, but he really had no other option.

Popping the doctor-prescribed pill into his mouth, Aditya began to think, *These auto guys are unbelievable. Fifty rupees for a two-kilometre ride?*

This autorickshaw cartel thing had been playing on his mind for quite some time.

Aditya was lost in his thoughts since he had come back from the hospital. Meena doubted if he had discussed about his illness properly with the doctor. She was only half-convinced when she noticed him popping in the medicines.

Sellers' Cartel! Aditya inferred again.

This was similar to what he had noticed in his own business. Any component that Aditya had bought in his business had a few sellers, and they formed a cartel – all the time.

Sellers usually gang up to form a cartel. The idea was to frame a set of basic rules of the game. Sellers competed only within the frame of rules that were conveniently designed for them.

Mulling over the topic of business cartels, he briskly walked from one end of his living room to another, several times, thinking intensely. He finally seemed to hit upon an idea!

Looking impatiently for his mobile phone, he called out, 'Meena?' But then he located the phone on the sofa.

Peeping into the living room, Meena found her husband calling someone from his mobile phone. She gestured to find what he had called her for. As if he was practising for some dumb charades, Aditya gestured that it was for his phone and looked happy that he had already found it.

Meena noticed a strange light glowing in his eyes and a remarkable change in her husband who looked more energetic now.

Did the pill start working so soon? she thought.

'Hi, Kannan,' said Aditya.

Understanding that Aditya had something official to discuss with Kannan, Meena disappeared into the kitchen.

'Yes, sir.'

'I need your help. You are the right person for this.'

'Sure.'

'Financially speaking, how is real estate business?'

Kannan did not expect that Aditya would think of a real estate business as his next venture. And that too, this quickly.

'Frankly, it is a very lousy business – financially.' Kannan had always shared a frank opinion with Aditya.

Kannan had worked with a small developer within Bengaluru before joining Kulkarni Metal Products. While he had worked there as an accountant for a short time, he picked up a lot of financial jugglery that his job entailed him to. During the initial days when he had worked with Uday, Aditya's father, he had complained in a lighter vein that his 'financial skills' were not exploited to their best. Uday's straightforward business and clean accounting was so boring for Kannan. Of course, he had no complaints for spending over seventeen years with Kulkarni Metal Products thereafter.

'Lousy? Why do you say that?' asked Aditya.

'Lousy, because, developers are always cash-challenged.'

'Cash-challenged? Why? No two-bedroom apartment in Bengaluru costs less than fifty lakhs today! With the cost of the land divided across hundreds of apartments, the cost to a developer should be pittance, no?'

'True. But they never get to use the cash coming from sales for building an apartment complex.'

'Then?'

'They would mortgage their apartments with banks and seek working capital for the construction.'

'But then what happens to the cash coming from the sales?'

'It goes to fund their strategic investments – the next land that they need. What will a developer do if he builds an apartment complex with all the cash coming in from sales? Yes, he will make some money. But if he waits until the project completion, he will have to shell out more money to buy a new land for the next project.'

'So he buys a new land every time he has sufficient cash from his existing projects?'

'Exactly. Remember, you always have bargaining power if you are buying a land on cash! So it works perfectly fine for a developer. Cash goes to fund your future investments. Bank loans fund your pending constructions!' summed up Kannan.

There was a pause from Aditya's side.

Growing suspicious on what Aditya's plan was, he added, 'Sir, please don't tell me that you are considering a real estate business venture.'

'No, I cannot be that silly.'

'Then what do you have on your mind?' asked Kannan very curiously. By that time, he sensed that Aditya had something else on his mind.

'Cartel. A Buyer's Cartel!'

'Sorry – can you please elaborate?'

Yes, Aditya was thinking about a buyers' cartel from the time he had returned from the hospital that day.

Consumers are always scattered, with each of them having unique requirements. They have no union of any sort – except for a few regulatory bodies that bring buyers together for resolving complaints on various products and services.

Aditya began to visualise the power of a buyers' cartel.

'Kannan, just think – what will happen if my neighbour and I decide not to hire an autorickshaw on our street?' asked Aditya.

'Just the two of you? It does not pinch anyone.'

'But what if all the families in the entire street decide not to hire any autorickshaw?'

'The auto guys waiting at the end of your street will be affected.'

'Good. And if the entire city decides to stop hiring an autorickshaw?'

This particular thought sent a shiver down Kannan's spine; he suddenly felt goosebumps.

The thought was so powerful that he could visualise auto guys panicking.

'Now, just imagine this – what if we manage to form a homebuyers' cartel and sit tight for a good bargain price. Frankly, how many of us can really afford a fifty to sixty lakh 2 BHK flat in Bengaluru?'

Kannan was the best person to visualise how the finance department of a developer would turn out to be if the sales dry up.

'Mind-boggling, sir! This will turn a developer upside down!'

Realising that Aditya had his eyes set on Singhania's real estate business in Bengaluru, he added, 'This can mark the beginning of the downfall of Singhania's real estate business.'

Aditya was visibly kicked up about the idea now. His eyes were radiant; he could feel a sudden rush of energy. He gripped his right-hand fist tightly.

'Yes!' he exclaimed and pumped his right hand in the air.

'But how will you do it?' asked Kannan.

CHAPTER 6
THE BIG PUSH

Looking through the window of his corner office and sipping on lemonade with kiwi syrup, Vivek seemed to rejoice in his position. Why not? Who would not envy a corner office in a business empire of his size? Who would not like a view from a towering structure in the business district of Bengaluru? An uninterrupted view from the tenth-floor office on MG Road would only be a matter of envy for others. And who would not cherish a few moments of silence that his business provides?

People imagine real estate business being quite hectic. But in reality, the big business plans of real estate companies would take shape rather very slowly. Everything takes time in this business – finding good sites for future projects, getting architects and engineers prepare blueprints, getting necessary approvals, and finally making apartments rise to the sky. And this is a business that owns a brand, and almost all other activities – from design to construction – are outsourced to partners. Real estate companies design the specifications of a brand, supervise the work for quality output, invite customers, and mint money as they sell each apartment. In the meantime, the business would provide plenty of time for a CEO like Vivek to sit silently in office, stare into infinity, sip some lemonade, and enjoy a few quiet moments.

A short but sharp beep coming in from Vivek's BlackBerry lying on the desk filled the silent room, jolting Vivek who had been soaked in the luxury of time by the window side. The phone then buzzed as it danced on the table to the incoming call in mute mode until he answered the call. It was Gaurav Singhania on the line.

'Sir?' said Vivek Mathur as nervously as he always would when Singhania makes such unscheduled phone calls.

'What's happening over there in Bengaluru, Vivek?'

Vivek wondered whether the question was a casual one or the one worthy enough to worry about.

'All fine, sir,' said Vivek hesitantly, keeping his response short.

'It is not fine,' said Singhania, proving Vivek's unexpressed doubt that something must have been wrong. 'I have been watching the CNBC. These guys are not at all talking about us. And you are running the fanciest business in my portfolio. What are you guys doing?' added Singhania.

Vivek was a little taken aback with Singhania's benchmark of his performance.

Are media stories my performance indicator? Vivek could not resist, but this thought was more than irritating. He wanted to break his head against the wall. Ever since he had joined this stock-market-listed company, he could not avoid but get measured on stock price movements and the amount of business visibility he gets on prime business channels.

Vivek decided to defend rather than duck the question. 'Sir, our Sarjapur Road project was covered by NDTV Hot Property last week. It should be coming on the TV in another fortnight. I was just waiting for the details from the NDTV team so that I can send them over to you.'

Seemingly unimpressed with his response, Singhania said, 'Vivek, think bigger. This visibility is certainly not good for you. If you are not launching new projects and if you are not covered by the media on your bigger plans, how will you expect your stock to perform well?'

'Sure sir, we will up our ante on our marketing programs.'

'Well, when are you launching your Koramangala and Nagarabhavi projects?' Singhania fired the next question.

'Sir?' Vivek swallowed, feeling uneasy.

'I disbursed sixty two crores for the two new projects and you seem to be clueless!' Singhania roared in his ears.

'Sorry, sir, I cannot hear you properly over the phone. Looks like I have some network issue,' said Vivek, trying to cover up the matter. 'Yes, the marketing brochures are ready.

The pre-launch offers on both the projects have been sent to the existing customers and investors. We are launching them on the next Friday, sir.'

'Fine – send me the brochures. What about the press conference and media ads?'

'Sir, the press conference is scheduled for the next Saturday. And the media ads are work in progress.'

'Faster, Vivek, faster. I need you to move much faster!' thundered Singhania and then murmured in a complaining, low tone, 'Stupid, *work in progress!*'

'Where are you on the township land acquisition?' asked Singhania.

Vivek realised that the no-show on CNBC had caused more damage than he had bargained for. Township project was a great task. Vivek said, 'Sir, I need some more time on this.'

'How many more days?' asked Singhania as if he gave him some concession.

Days? Vivek asked himself. He ideally needed another month to finalise. His team still had no proposed site on the Outer Ring Road where Singhania was expecting them to find.

'Sir, we will propose something very soon,' said Vivek, intelligently circumventing a potential deadline.

'Give me a specific date – I will wait,' Singhania persisted. Vivek knew that Singhania could turn this adamant and uncompromising if he had decided to. Vivek wondered why bosses were so tough to deal with.

'May I take some time – till end of this month?'

'Sorry, take ten days. I will wait.'

Vivek wanted to scream, *Ten days? Big deal! Didn't you say you will take my proposed date?* But he did not say that. He could not afford to say that. He might be the CEO of the company, but that would cost him his job.

Getting skittish with a faster deadline, Vivek chose not to respond or accept the new deadline. It would be near impossible for his team to identify an 80-100 acre land for the township project in ten more days. He certainly would need more time than that.

Realising that Vivek paused on the phone, Singhania added, 'Vivek, I am not sure if you understand the importance of the township project. We cannot sit and watch the bigger guys in this market launch and walk away with their township projects. We are already late in this game. But we need to make a bigger and better impact than others. If you are successful with one mega township project, I will take care of you.'

Singhania was always good in offering carrots and sticks. Unfortunately, Vivek was used to more of his sticks than the carrots.

'Yes, sir. I see what you are saying. We will propose a good site for the township,' said Vivek and then added after a pause, 'shortly.'

'Not shortly. Within ten days.' Singhania immediately disconnected the call.

Vivek dropped his phone on the table and looked around in his cabin. The dark glass opposite him reflected his image – his face had turned red. The business pressure was mounting these days. He gazed through the window and threw his hands up in the air in frustration. He would need a miracle to find a good 80-100 acre land in the next ten days.

He picked up the lemonade and sipped again. The drink suddenly seemed to taste bad.

CHAPTER 7

THE FACEBOOK IDEA

Stretching on the sofa after dinner, Aditya switched on the TV. The channel that popped up was a prime Hindi channel featuring a musical contest. A contestant crooned with all his energy as he sung the last few lines of a popular song. The audience erupted in a thunderous clamour as the singer finished the song in style.

'*Beta*, you have disappointed me,' said a judge.

The contestant looked unhappy for a second, but the TV frame was frozen for several seconds, tilting the singer's picture in three odd angles and shattering background music animated the ambience.

'*Aapka* landing notes *yeh na, aaj tho bahut jagah* flat *hogaya hai*,' added the judge. (In many instances, your landing notes were flat today.)

This time, the TV frame froze other contestants in a daze and an otherwise happy audience shocked.

Is this a musical show or a drama? thought Aditya and flipped through other channels.

Aditya stopped by the raucous on a prime time, nine o' clock news channel. There were about six people on the TV frame with the anchor at the centre, and with each of the participant's location mentioned below their video frame.

'But why?' screamed the news anchor.

'Abhijit, we cannot exactly explain the reason why none of the policemen checked the terrace,' said a senior police officer.

'But why?' repeated the anchor.

'Abhijit, this is a murder case, and the case is being investigated. I cannot discuss what is still being investigated. We need to wait until the findings are out,' replied the police officer.

'At what time did the victim's father make the last call and to whom?' asked the anchor.

Four others on the show began to speak all at once after the police officer had said, '3 a.m.'

Raising his voice and requesting the others to stay calm, the news anchor said, 'You tell me, Mr Chopra, as a leading psychiatrist in the country, what's your analysis? Why will a guy make a phone call at 3 a.m., at such wee hours, to a person whom . . .'

Another drama! What does he think about himself? Is he a news analyst or a private detective? Aditya asked himself before switching off the TV.

When the picture on the TV screen zoomed in and vanished with a press of the red button, the cacophony in that room died.

Peaceful, thought Aditya.

Arriving on the first floor, Aditya noticed Meena and his son were busy playing with his laptop.

'What are you guys doing?' asked Aditya curiously.

'I am helping him go through Sachin's Facebook community page,' said Meena.

Meena was the one who introduced Aditya to Facebook about a year ago. She had connected with her school and college friends over Facebook and was happy to catch up with their lives. She had posted a few of her old school photographs and showed Aditya how many *Likes* those pictures gathered over the next two days. Aditya had initially thought that Meena was too childlike to spend so much time posting photographs, expecting comments, and rechecking her page every few hours in the evenings. But when she had finally persuaded Aditya to open his own page and find his friends online, he had realised the power of technology. With a few clicks, to his amazement, he found that he could share his stuff with the world. There was no necessity to remember the email ids of all his friends.

'Sachin Tendulkar's community on Facebook?' asked Aditya.

'Yes, there is a Facebook community on Sachin Tendulkar. We are *friends* of this community. The community posts photos and videos of Sachin's best shots from various games.'

Leaning towards the laptop monitor, Aditya curiously noticed the screen.

'Look here, *appa*. There are 2.5 million Sachin *friends* who *Like* this page!' added his son.

'2.5 million?' Aditya's voice indicated that he was surprised of such a big number.

'*Appa*, that's not big at all. There are several such communities with millions and millions of *friends* worldwide.'

'But what do you do here?' asked Aditya curiously.

'If I like a picture, I hit *Like*,' said his son, showing the *Like* button on the screen, 'and if I have a comment, I post it here.'

Courtesy Meena, Aditya was familiar with these features already. But that day, Aditya was curious on finding how community pages were different from individual profiles.

'But how do you start a community?'

'Very simple. You select this "create a page" and select a "community". That's it!' Meena demonstrated enthusiastically.

Thanks to Meena again, Aditya got exactly what he needed now.

'Can you please leave the laptop for me now? I have something important and urgent to complete.'

His son uninterestingly complied, and as he rose from the seat, Meena signalled him to sleep in the adjacent bedroom.

Aditya began viewing his homepage on Facebook. He had a few updates on his private message board.

'Any good news?' asked Jürgen from United Petro.

'I have some bad news and good news. The bad news is that I lost my business and almost everything else in life. But the good news is that I am determined to bring down the empire of Singhania. Very shortly, I am going to demonstrate the power of silence to Singhania!' Aditya dropped a cryptic response to Jürgen.

'Any update?' asked Prof. Srinivas from Chennai. Aditya sent a similar response to him.

The private message inbox had another message. This was from Shaji. 'Sir, I got a job in Renuka Steels Pvt. Ltd. in Peenya industrial area. I will be taking care of the entire production here. I am glad to share this good news from my side. I have been thinking about you – how are you doing?'

'Fantastic! Smart people will always get a good job. Wishing you the very best in your new assignment. I am sure you will do a great job. I am doing fine. I have a great idea to crumble Singhania's real estate business. Please watch out your inbox – you will receive a related message shortly. Looking forward to your cooperation!' replied Aditya to Shaji's message.

Clearing his inbox, Aditya was then all set to launch his bazooka on Singhania's real estate business in Bengaluru.

Just as Meena had demonstrated, he started a new Facebook community on the web. He named it – The Coolest Real Estate Brigade.

His first public message on the wall said, 'Dear Friends, here is the most *sakkat* real estate offer ever – get a flat 40 per cent discount on any Bengaluru residential property! No, I am not kidding.' *Sakkat* in Kannada means excellent.

Aditya then added to his wall message, 'Here is a set of nine simple but very tough conditions that you need to accept and comply with.

In the next two years:

1. Make no phone calls to any developer in Bengaluru – ever
2. Visit no residential property in Bengaluru – ever
3. Don't fall for attractive offers or agree for a *free* site visit. Politely reject the offers and say, "No, thank you – I am not looking for any property."
4. Don't ever search for a property on websites – be it sulekha.com, magicbricks.com, 99acres.com, or other favourites
5. Never attend any realty expositions/exhibitions in Bengaluru
6. Don't be a proxy to your NRI friends or family members in evaluating residential properties on their behalf

7. You should have your family members comply with these conditions and also encourage your NRI friends or associates to join this group

8. Please report your compliance with the above seven simple rules once in every fortnight

9, You should send your full name, contact number, your residential requirement, preferred locations to buy a property in Bengaluru and your budget – you may please send this information in a private message, for your own privacy reasons

Let me reiterate: The above nine rules might appear simple, but they are very tough to comply with. But if you manage to stay in compliance with these rules for the next two years, here is the guarantee that you will be provided with a flat 40 per cent discount on today's residential prices anywhere in Bengaluru.'

Aditya further added, 'Please do not underestimate the power of one. You will never be alone if you religiously follow these nine simple rules. Embrace the power of silence and get your 40 per cent offer. There cannot be another *sakkat* offer than this!'

Aditya reread the message and recognised a need to convince *non-believers*. He then appended the message, 'If you don't believe that this will work, please try this: get a complete consensus that no one in your apartment complex will hire any autorickshaw parked nearby for at least one month. I am sure you get snubbed by their arrogant deals. Let the consensus in your apartment complex be to reject hiring as well as to completely ignore their services, if offered. Please see how the power of silence will play out in strict compliance from everyone!'

Hitting 'share' button, Aditya tagged this information with 200 of his contacts on Facebook.

Aditya then drafted a similar email with a request to join the Facebook community and also forward the email only to their known contacts who wanted to buy a home in Bengaluru.

CHAPTER 8
A SHOT IN THE ARM

S inghania was getting ready – preparing for a review meeting with Debojit Sengupta, CEO of Singhania Power, and his team. They apparently had some news of great significance to discuss.

The meeting was about to start in another five minutes and then his phone began to ring.

'Yes, Vivek. What's up?'

'Sir, I have some good news for you.' Vivek sounded very excited over phone.

'Go ahead!'

'We sent you an option to consider for our township project by email. I am happy that the deal has come out very attractive for us.'

'What's the deal? How much land did you manage to find?'

'Sir, this is a 85-acre land – right on the Outer Ring Road, just as you suggested us to explore. This land is near BEL circle – strategically positioned in North Bengaluru, nicely located from the proposed Bengaluru Metro's hub.'

'But how is the deal?'

'I am coming to that, sir. We have managed to close the deal at 700 crores!' Vivek cried out happily.

'Good show, Vivek!' congratulated Singhania.

Working to about eight crores per acre, this was an unbelievable deal that Singhania could ever imagine to close. If one were to consider the market rates, it should have been priced at a minimum of 1,200 crores. Singhania's team had managed to close it at nearly 50 per cent discount. And it had very conveniently worked out for him to let his team close the deal within ten days.

His pressure on the team had worked wonders, Singhania inferred.

'Good show, Vivek,' Singhania repeated his praise without a second thought. He then curiously asked, 'How did you do it?'

Vivek was pushed so hard by Singhania that he had to resort to mean business tactics. After taking several months of planning and executing the Whitefield land-grabbing, Vivek had lost his patience. Singhania's ten days ultimatum had pushed him into a corner.

Vivek had sent a team of goons to close the deal at gunpoint, championing a new, nasty era of bringing Mumbai's mafia to Bengaluru's real estate. Sacrificing his reputation, he had to resort to this since he had joined the Singhania Group as there was no Singhania kind of overambitious boss earlier in his career. He feared of being sacked from the job more these days than any other time in his career.

There is no point in explaining the means of closing the deal this time, Vivek thought.

Answering with a chuckle, he instead said, 'It was a happy ending, sir.' Vivek could have qualified it as *forced happy ending*, but he did not.

'Whatever. You seem to have got your tricks right! This is the time you chill. Bye!'

Vivek was completely relieved with the expected praise coming in.

'Bye, sir.'

Singhania got a shot in the arm. He wanted something like this for quite some time now. He wanted a large canvas to paint a grand picture – large enough to grab the attention of his investors and the media.

This was it. Singhania rejoiced in a moment of achievement as an 85-acre plot was good enough to announce his grand entry to fairly large residential cum commercial township projects.

Realising that he was getting late to the review meeting with Singhania Power team, he then rushed to the conference room where the team was already waiting.

'Good morning, sir.' The team stood on their feet, in the trademark way to start his meetings.

'Very good morning, folks!'

Looking at a happy Singhania, the team was half convinced that he had gone through the report that they had submitted for his perusal.

Taking his seat, Singhania threw the file on the table in front and opened it. The first document in the file was titled, 'The largest discovery of uranium in India.'

'Debojit, I did glance through this interesting development. What's your take on this?' Singhania kickstarted the meeting.

'Sir, this discovery at Tummalapalle in Andhra Pradesh is the biggest breakthrough in our country. While it is estimated that this reserve might have 49,000 tonnes of uranium, our sources say that there is more to it. That way, this will not only be the largest uranium reserve in India, but the largest discovery in the entire world!'

In all his excitement, Debojit added, 'This will reduce our dependency to import uranium for nuclear power. India can instead export it. And our . . .'

Cutting him short, Singhania interrupted, 'But what are your inferences for Singhania Power?'

'Sir, with significant increase in Indian nuclear power production in the future, we can focus on scaling up our equipment . . .'

'What about mining?' Singhania interrupted again.

He probably knew what Debojit wanted to tell: that this could encourage them to scale up their nuclear power equipment business.

'Sir?' asked Debojit.

'When will we get the mining license?' thundered Singhania. He suddenly turned very serious for reasons that Debojit could not guess.

Uranium mining was restricted to only a government agency appointed for this activity. While Singhania and other large power producers had lobbied for opening up the uranium mining sector for the private players, it fell on deaf ears. Private players could neither directly produce nuclear power nor mine the raw material. Private players could only provide ancillary components and services to the public sector companies.

'Sir, you very well know that we have been running pillar to post. Ministry folks are not letting us get the right appointments.'

'How long, Debojit?' said Singhania frustratingly. 'This has been going on for several years. I doubt if you are using the right methods to reach out and lobby with the ministry.'

'Sir, we have budgeted for all things that will keep our ministers happy. But the talks never reached advanced stages,' complained Debojit.

'What's the use in budgeting and keeping the money in our bank? Throw some money at them. Who's sane in this country? But I cannot wait for long!' Singhania expressed his disappointment with the progress of the uranium mining license.

There was a brief pause. Debojit preferred to remain silent rather than talk around in circles and get beaten down to death.

Breaking the silence, Singhania added, 'If we keep watching discovery after discovery, we will only let the public sector folks to freak out. We missed the discoveries in Karnataka and Bihar in the past. And now, this Andhra Pradesh discovery – largest in the world! The news that you brought to me today is, in fact, very bad news for us. We missed it – one more time.'

Singhania's anger was visible. His eyes had popped out, his eyebrows arched, and his lips stiffened as he said those words.

Trying to tone down the discussion, Debojit said, 'Sir, we will intensify our lobbying.'

'You should. There is no other way out. This government has sufficient majority in the Parliament. Join hands with our competitors, make the team bigger, or whatever it takes. But I need our lobby to work faster. I need to see the government talking about the uranium mining bill by this winter session. You understand that?' Singhania's voice was so intense that it was echoing in the boardroom which was otherwise perfectly insulated.

'Yes, sir.'

'Please learn ways to bring the government into your pocket, my friend!'

'I shall give my 100 per cent, sir.'

'Then how is our nuclear power equipment business doing?' asked Singhania, moving to the next agenda item on the meeting.

'Sir, our joint venture with Pouvoir de France SA is shaping up very well. My team feels that our investment of 950 crores in jointly developing nuclear reactors, cooling systems, precision components cannot be more perfect. Our order book is massively increasing – sitting at the moment at over 2,500 crores for the next three years. In another six to seven months, we will be delivering two reactors and cooling systems at Silluru Nuclear Power plant and another two sets at Shindra Nuclear Power plant.'

Located in the southern tip of Andhra Pradesh near Sriharikota, Silluru Nuclear Power plant had planned production of 3,000 MW of power. This plant could be one of the biggest beneficiaries of the recent uranium discovery at Tummalapalle. With the proximity of the raw material, the proposed scale of production might also increase.

The Shindra Nuclear Power plant was located in the Kutch region of Gujarat. The location was strategically chosen to provide access to Kandla and Mundra ports nearby. The proposed production here was 3,500 MW, making it one of the biggest nuclear power plants in the country.

'When are Silluru and Shindra plants getting commissioned by the government?'

'Sir, they are running on schedule. They should be commissioned by the next May as per plan.'

'Good, the government will understand how different it is to outsource building nuclear power plants to the private sector.'

Singhania's inference was probably right. There were some nuclear power plants in India that had witnessed significant delays and were yet to be commissioned even after a decade of their planned completion. Technology was rudimentary and execution was poor without private sector participation.

With foreign collaboration and import of technology know-how, Singhania and other large private sector players began to demonstrate their superior capability. By finalising the joint venture with Pouvoir de France SA, Singhania had managed to get one of the best partners in the world. France was by far the best country that had demonstrated the success of nuclear power – 75 per cent of France's power requirement today was addressed through nuclear power.

After a brief pause, Singhania added, 'So we have less than one year to commission the power plants?'

'Yes, sir.'

'How are we doing on the hydro and thermal power businesses?' The expression on Singhania's face said that this was a very causal question. He did not really care about Debojit's response. Singhania was aware that there was nothing much to review here. It was business as usual.

'Sir, the last two quarters have been excellent for us on thermal power. Our profit margins are slated to go up by 3 per cent because of abundant availability of coal. The coal price was at an all-time low, and we lifted enormous amount of stock to take advantage of the low prices. The hydro power generation was also uninterrupted. Good monsoon this year is showing up in our reservoirs, and I am glad that our turbines are busy – round the clock!'

'How will the numbers come out on hydro business for this quarter?'

'Sir, we will demonstrate a net sales growth of 15 per cent. Profitability is intact.'

'Fine. I am not too much worried about this part of your business. Even you know that. But I need our nuclear power business to scale up. You need to accelerate our lobbying for uranium mining. Once mining is opened up for the private sector, we can lobby for nuclear power generation. The world will then know who Singhania is!'

'Sure, sir. We will be on that job. We will make our flag fly high!' Debojit conveniently added some English that made Singhania swell with pride.

'Good show!'

CHAPTER 9
ANOTHER SHOT IN THE ARM

Meena had come laughing to Aditya who was sipping his morning coffee and reading a magazine. She opened out the *World View* section of *The Economic Times* and pointed to the Dilbert comic strip at the bottom of the page.

In this strip, Wally, a lead character that personifies an unquenchable American thirst for coffee, was shown approached by a guy who carried a piece of paper and asked, 'Wally, would you . . .'

Wally responded, 'No, I'm doing something important for the brand integration manager.'

'Maybe after that you could . . .'

'Then I'm doing a rush job for the director of sustainability,' answered Wally.

'Are those even real people?' asked the guy naively.

'Welcome to the Matrix Management, Neo,' said Wally.

Aditya laughed out loud.

'Welcome to the Matrix Management, Neo,' Aditya read aloud and laughed again.

Bursting into laughter, Meena observed Aditya laughing and felt happy. It had been months since she had seen him laughing his heart out.

'Good one,' said Aditya.

Knowing Aditya had always liked the Dilbert strip, Meena tried her bit to keep the fun alive.

'You look good when you laugh,' said Meena.

'Thank you.'

Aditya realised how subtly Meena would manage to keep him lively.

'How is our Facebook community doing? Did you check?' asked Meena.

'I checked it the last week. Well, let me check it now.'

It was nearly a month since Aditya had started the Facebook community of The Coolest Real estate Brigade.

Aditya enthusiastically opened the website. Even before he could check for new Facebook Wall updates, his mobile began to ring.

'Hi, Pratap, how are you doing?'

'Fine. And you?'

'Fine. What's the news?'

'Hmm . . . guess what, I started a business on my own.'

'Great. What's that?'

'What else could be a cool business for a HR guy? I have turned a head-hunter now. In the last one month, I had numerous meetings with my HR fraternity all over Bengaluru and Mumbai. People are open to business. There is no retainer in this business. But if I manage to find the right profile for my clients, I will get paid very handsomely.'

'Fantastic, Pratap. I am very happy for you.'

'And you know what – I get to work out of home!'

'That's cool.'

'Yes, all I need is my mobile, a table and chair, and my laptop with an internet connection.'

'I am sure that your family loves this arrangement more than you do.' Aditya laughed out heartily.

'You bet!'

'I am happy that your rich experience is coming in handy like this. But I hope I did not throw you out into a wild sea.' Aditya's voice had a sincere tone of concern.

'No, sir. Everything happens for a good reason.'

Aditya repeated it in his mind: *Everything happens for a good reason.*

Pratap was perhaps right, but he was not sure. What had happened to him was unimaginable and unexpected. There had been several days in the recent past when Aditya had questioned why someone wanted to conspire against him. And against him alone! He had no immediate answers, but he hoped to find an answer soon.

Like the great poet Kabir said, *You don't pray to God unless you get into trouble*, Aditya began praying to God more sincerely in the previous one month than he had ever before. When the life was good, his daily short prayers were very customary. But in previous few days, he often lost into long hours of spiritual thoughts.

'Everything happens for a good reason,' repeated Aditya. 'You are probably right. But I am yet to find the reason why God let such a devastating thing happen.'

'I'm sorry. Please don't get me wrong, but I think there is a merit in avoiding any judgement on any event. Why should you treat someone grabbing your property as negative?' asked Pratap.

Aditya was in a daze for a moment. *It was indeed a devastating event for him.*

Gently persuading Aditya, Pratap added, 'Just pause and mull over the subject and ask yourself – is it really a negative event . . . ?'

It was indeed a pertinent question to ponder about. Aditya began to think. The fallout of the incident was indeed negative. He lost his business, money, and peace of mind. But was it enough to call it a *negative event*?

Pratap added, 'Take my case. You can say that I lost my job. Then whatever happened to me can be considered "negative". But I asked one question to myself – is this an opportunity to start something on my own? I felt if I cannot start now, I will probably never ever start anything in my life. Then I realised that this incident is indeed "positive". Now, I am starting this new venture with a completely positive energy.'

Pratap's words began to sink in. He seemed to have some enchanted words for him. Aditya heard him keenly.

'Look no further than Ramayana, Aditya. When Ravana abducted Sita, it would have been a devastating event for Lord Rama. This event happened within a short time after Rama was banished to the forests for fourteen years – which, in turn, had happened when he was supposed to have been crowned as the king of *Ayodhya*. But only because Sita was abducted, Rama had an opportunity to meet Hanuman, his greatest disciple, and made several new friends thereafter. Only because Sita was abducted, Rama had an opportunity to engineer *Ramsethu*, a bridge to Lanka that would have helped the mankind afterwards. Only because Sita was abducted, Rama had a chance to kill Ravana, an *asura* who thought he was invincible.'

Aditya listened raptly to those words which were a ballast of strength. Aditya wondered if Pratap had brought this out of the epic books as a perfect analogy, but it seemed so: if he were to be Rama, his lost love was his business, and the Ravana of his life was Singhania. He, therefore, had to see to it that Singhania lost this *war of dharma*.

Giving a sincere advice, Pratap added, 'Instead of judging the incident, simply experience the current state of affairs. I believe that every event offers us a lesson. Maybe you will discover the lesson very soon in this seemingly negative and devastating event.'

Pratap was indeed a personal guide and philosopher at the office. This magical approach to various situations in the past had helped numerous individual workers and Kulkarni Metal Products, as a company, in general. That day, Aditya was experiencing that magic. In the last few minutes, he had gained tremendous power to deal with the reality.

'Pratap, let me tell you that you certainly have some magic. I really hope I will come out of this crisis very soon,' said Aditya.

'Don't worry, sir. You will do well. This is the other reason why I called you.'

Pausing for a while, Pratap added, 'I have been following and promoting your Facebook community. I shared it with fifteen of my HR friends in Bengaluru. Each one of them was looking to buy an apartment. They now believe in you and your determination to sit tight for a good deal. They not only joined the online community but have apparently sent this information to numerous employees that they know in their companies. Did you get to see any action for yourself?'

'Wow, that's great. I have just logged on to the Facebook community and then I received your call. I checked the online activity a week ago. I had twenty-six *Likes* and was happy to see all twenty-six people sharing their contact details.'

'It is nice to know that. I will try and promote this more actively. My travel within Bengaluru and to Mumbai will be more limited now. I will have more free time. I already have some business on hand. Now all I need is a little time to find the right people for the current client requirements.'

'Great. I really appreciate your support. I will check on the Facebook activity now. Thank you.'

'Bye, sir.'

'Bye.'

Aditya immediately turned his attention to the online community. The Facebook community wall was pouring messages!

He glanced on the left side of the page. It indicated that as of that particular day, the community had 137 Likes! This was phenomenal activity in just under one week – an increase of 427 per cent in the investor base that was willing to postpone their purchase decision by two years.

Aditya quickly checked a few messages. He had eighty-nine private messages. The first four to five messages clearly indicated that all the rest of the private messages had contact details of various people registered with the community. Meanwhile, he found that there were more bold people who shared their mobile numbers and their requirements right on the community's public Wall. In all happiness, Aditya concurrently opened an Excel file to record the new registrations.

Aditya spent the next half hour recording the new registrations, 137 potential investors in all, into his Excel file. He jumped and smiled in delight after seeing such overwhelming response and community activity.

Putting Pratap on a speed dial, Aditya said, 'Pratap, it's working! 137 registrations so far. Over 400 per cent increase in the registrations compared to the last week!'

'Excellent!'

'Thank you. I will call you again later. I need to share this good news with Kannan too!'

Pratap knew how fondly Aditya was associated with Kannan. They had a great chemistry.

'Kannan, there is a great development. We have 137 Likes on the Facebook community. Can you imagine 137 potential investors registering in one month? They all chose to sit silent for the next two years.'

'This is really good news. I am sure this is just the beginning!'

'By the way, what's the news with you?'

'I just landed from Mumbai this morning with a good job opportunity. I might be joining Indian National Bank. They are looking for a finance manager for their broking business in Bengaluru.'

'Congrats, I am very happy for you. And you know what, just a while ago, Pratap mentioned that he has started something on his own. He has turned a head hunter.'

'Is it? That's very good news. I should probably check if there are any better options for me!' Kannan chuckled. 'I am yet to receive their offer letter.'

'Yep, why not? Seriously, give him a call and find if you have any better options.'

Aditya heard a beep indicating an incoming call as he spoke with Kannan. Looking at the screen, he noted that it was Shaji. He closed the call with Kannan with customary wishes.

'Hi, Shaji. How are you?' asked Aditya, answering the incoming call.

'Sir, I am doing fine. I have some information for you. I am not sure, how useful it will be, though.'

'What's that?'

'Singhania Realty is the biggest customer for Renuka Steels. Nearly 80 per cent of the production is consumed by Singhania's residential properties in Bengaluru. I have learnt this from our sales head. Just two days ago, we have moved a massive stock to Singhania's Koramangala and Nagarabhavi projects.'

'OK. It seems his construction activities are in full swing.'

'Yes, sir.'

'Please keep a tab on the stock that is moving to his projects. I will talk to you later for more updates.'

'Sure, sir.'

'Thank you very much. This is indeed a great piece of information from you.'

Aditya was overwhelmed with the information that had come to him that day: a 400 per cent jump in Facebook registrations, Pratap's beginning as a head hunter, Kannan's joining the Indian National Bank, and then Shaji's information on Singhania's purchase of steel.

The last bit of news troubled him a little, though. A 400 per cent increase in investors on Facebook might be great news for him, but he realised that in absolute terms, 137 people in Bengaluru were not even a pinch for Singhania.

Probably, Aditya would need this stellar performance of the community to continue for a few more months. Only then he could see some effect.

CHAPTER 10
WHERE IS THE MINING
LICENSE?

One month later . . .

Singhania was in his palatial corporate office room, watching CNBC-TV 18.

'With the prices of coal and crude falling, what sectors are you tracking, Mr Mehta?' asked the lady on the channel.

'Sonali, we particularly like the power sector, which is the biggest beneficiary of the falling coal prices. The price of coal is at multiyear lows, and at this kind of levels, there is always pent-up demand from the power producers. We also see imports going up, bringing cheaper coal from Indonesia, if these price levels sustain for a few more weeks.'

'Any interesting picks in the power sector, Mr Mehta?'

'A disclaimer to start with – we have Bansal Power in the large cap space and PST Power from the midcap space. Bansal is particularly looking good as they have captive mines to leverage. The company has increased the production capacity in the last three quarters.'

'And why do you like PST Power?' asked the anchor.

Singhania turned red-faced. *Why are they not talking about Singhania Power?* he thought.

Over the next few minutes, the news anchor steered the conversation in discovering some multi-bagger stocks in the power and capital goods sectors. The analyst, to Singhania's fury, either mentioned the top three or some obscure, smaller players in each of the businesses.

It was over a month since Debojit and his team had left with a promise to expedite the uranium mining lobbying. There was no update from the team since then.

The last fifteen-minute TV show and the continuously running ticker on CNBC had enough effect to unsettle Singhania.

Picking up his mobile phone, Singhania immediately called Debojit.

'Good morning, sir.'

'Not a good one for me!'

Debojit was a little taken aback by the blunt, opening remark. He grappled for what to say now. Instead of saying something, he chose to remain silent and get a clue to what Singhania had on his mind.

'What's the progress on the uranium mining? Did you meet the minister?'

Debojit was zapped with these questions coming his way. One month was no way sufficient to update on the progress of lobbying for a new mining bill. It was not like a regular sales order or government tender process. He certainly needed more time on this.

'Sir . . .' Debojit invariably dragged and deliberated on what to say as he began to speak.

'I need a clear answer. I am listening,' demanded Singhania.

'Sir, Akshay has been camping in Delhi. He is still there.' Akshay was the public relations officer at Singhania Power.

'What the hell is he doing there in Delhi?'

Debojit grappled for an answer, again.

What else would a public relations officer do in Delhi? he asked himself. He had sent him about a month ago on the uranium mining assignment with the ministry.

'The mining minister is in Davos today! And our Akshay must be enjoying at his home,' thundered Singhania.

Debojit received a jolt! Fumbling a little, he said, 'I am very sorry, sir.'

'Debojit, I am really stunned at the level of information that you are on top of. You seem to have no clue on the Economic Summit at Davos!'

Debojit turned pale in embarrassment. He knew about Davos Summit, but his mind went blank from the very first remark that Singhania had made that day. He was still wondering why Singhania was so upset that morning.

Still fumbling a little, Debojit said, 'I know, sir. But . . .'

'This drama has been going on for several months, Debojit. You cannot even get one meeting with the minister. I will have to wait for my entire life to open up the uranium mining business for us. You need to know where to catch hold of our ministers better. Look, here is an action item for you.'

'Sir?'

'I am going to send you a number of a lady, Nisha Buckley. She runs a PR firm out of Switzerland. She is a specialist – corporate lobbyist. I got her reference from one of the best guys in our industry. She is at the moment camping in a presidential suite in a hotel in Davos. Please call her immediately and explain our case. She apparently has the mobile numbers of who's who that we need. Taking the foreign mobile number of the minister, you need to schedule a dinner appointment with her.' Pausing for a second, Singhania added, 'And you got to do that right now!'

'Sir . . .' said Debojit, wondering who this new lady was.

'What are you thinking? Nisha Buckley is born to an Indian mother and a French father,' said Singhania as if he read his mind. 'I looked at her photograph. She looks stunning, and I hear that she can get things done in her own style. I will be glad if her lip service for us and some hip service to the ministers work in our favour. But be sure that you schedule the dinner appointment tonight.'

'Yes, sir.' Debojit was now clear. Singhania had managed to reduce him, the CEO of a company, to a pimp. He had no other option but to do what Singhania wanted him to.

'What is your PR budget for this year?' asked Singhania out of the blue.

'Twenty-three crores, sir.'

'Please go for double that expense and consider that approved! A presidential suite in Switzerland and a hot chic would not come cheap. It is probably much better than wasting money on guys who travel to Delhi when the entire ministry is in Davos. Bye.'

The closing remarks from Singhania sounded as if he gave one tight slap on Debojit's cheek. It was a very bad day for him.

Within seconds of closing the call, Debojit's BlackBerry had an incoming message. Singhania had promptly sent the contact number of Nisha. *Nisha Buckley*, he reminded himself of the immediate task.

PART III

A TRICKLE

CHAPTER 11
6714 SOLDIERS

Three more months later . . .

Aditya clutched the locked gates of Kulkarni Metal Products at Whitefield. It was more than six months since he had lost his property.

He noticed that the lock on the main gate carried a court seal, and the lawyer's notice still stuck on the factory compound wall. On the left side of the main gate, the deserted factory campus had overgrown weeds, what looked like tall grass, in place of perfectly manicured garden. The grass had grown too high but looked pale and dry. The reception and administrative blocks that were otherwise visible through the main gate were now less visible through the tall grass. On to the right side of the compound wall, an array of trees stood lifeless, with most of their leaves shed. The pathway that ran around the factory campus was completely strewn with dried leaf litter.

He felt a lump building in his throat when he saw his factory in such a neglected condition.

Thinking about his father and looking up into the sky, he said to himself, *He must be cursing me for letting this go.*

If everything were to be normal, this factory would have been buzzing with machinery running throughout the day and people working all around the factory buildings. Right now, every worker who had contributed to that buzz was gone. And every machine that had worked like a running-train turned dead silent. It was eerily silent inside the factory premises.

At this moment, his heart craved for the life that he had enjoyed earlier – for a life that was presented by his father, for a life that was stolen by a hedonistic businessman.

He knew that a mere mission of bringing down Singhania's business empire would not be enough. He needed to win this factory back – faster than otherwise possible, earlier than any residential project which could come up here.

How do I get this back? He asked the same question for the last six months without a clear answer. Nevertheless, he needed to find an answer before it was too late.

'How is your Facebook community doing?' asked Meena when Aditya was back at home.

'It's doing fine. I see the momentum building up. We had some 4,200 members a fortnight ago,' said Aditya.

'Very good. Are you doing anything specific to keep up the momentum?'

'No. Not really.'

'I am just curious. What activities are carried out online?'

'There are quite a lot of discussions going on. People have been posting their observations, comments, compliance updates and so on.'

'I have a suggestion,' said Meena. 'Why don't you call everyone for a meeting? I suppose you would also need a better connection with them to build trust and a personal touch.'

'Wow!' exclaimed Aditya. 'That's a great idea. Maybe I should find some place on the outskirts of Bengaluru to accommodate everyone.'

'Yes, I feel it will work in our favour.'

Aditya could not appreciate Meena more for such an idea. She was intelligent and sensible, supporting him in whatever way possible.

'Thank you for this idea. Let's check the Facebook activity right now and propose it.'

Aditya immediately logged on to the Facebook community page. He could not believe his eyes – the community had 6714 *Likes!* That was a 60 per cent increase in the number of people registered in want of a residential flat at 40 per cent discount within a fortnight. Meanwhile, he found that his private message inbox was flooded with messages.

To satisfy the growing curiosity, Aditya opened a few profiles of people who registered recently. Four out of the first five names that he clicked worked with Wipro, Infosys, or TCS. Ten out of the next fourteen that he checked were also from some of these companies or from other software companies like HP, IBM, or Accenture.

He was thrilled with what he had seen.

Aditya had worked in the manufacturing industry for a long time, and it was not easy for him to understand what constituted Bengaluru's consumption. This market was dominated by software professionals for over fifteen years now. Had it not been a software hub, Bengaluru would have remained as it was – essentially a large town with individual houses and mediocre consumer spending led by government employees and retired professionals. But thanks to the software boom, Bengaluru had witnessed the rise of hundreds of apartment complexes. Mall after mall, more than a dozen in the recent past, had become extremely popular with the younger folks and had seen increased spending of these working professionals.

Even before Aditya could realise, he had hit upon a formula that could click with the demographics of Bengaluru. The city's young software professionals were the most active netizens – blogging, tweeting, or updating their Facebook Walls. Round the clock. An email in Bengaluru could travel hundred times faster than it would take in any other city in India.

When Bengaluru's demographics stand in favour of a revolutionary idea that Aditya was nurturing, the time had finally come! Didn't someone say that no one could stop an idea whose time had come?

This was it – Aditya was waiting for a response like this. This was an overwhelming response.

Aditya noticed that the Facebook Wall had hundreds of messages, many with compliance status to the nine rules of the offer; some had contact details of the newly registered people. But there was one message that caught his attention.

The message said, 'I am sorry to inform that my compliance to the nine rules of this community was broken today. My wife called up a developer to get more information on their newspaper advertisement. We had a big fight after that but we ended it after I opened and showed this Facebook page for her. It was my mistake that I did not take her into confidence. She wanted to convey her apologies for the non-compliance. She has now resolved to stay absolutely quiet until we get our dream home, a 2 BHK at a FLAT 40 per cent discount.'

This message alone had 4,200 *Likes*! There were many comments in this message chain that consistently had a similar message: 'Aditya, please allow him to get a 40 per cent discount.'

Aditya had tears of happiness in his eyes.

In the war that he had launched on Singhania, today he was not alone. He had 6714 soldiers – a set of 6714 determined homebuyers who had decided to postpone their home purchase by two years, a pair of 6714 hands which thumped and demanded an incredible offer, a pair of 6714 feet that began to march away and not towards Singhania, and a brigade of 6714 soldiers that might very soon leave Singhania confused and bewildered.

Aditya could not expect a better response than this in such a short time.

Even before he could completely digest this message chain, there was another message that caught his attention.

This message said, 'I was sceptical about the whole idea initially. I had resigned from the idea that my lonely silent war against heated-up residential prices was not worth fighting. But deep down, somewhere I was a little sceptical, and I have tried what Aditya had suggested us to.

My residential apartment in Malleshwaram is remotely located. The nearest bus stop is a little over two kilometres away. We used to have six to seven autorickshaws waiting, at any time, right at our main gate. I have managed to bring the entire residents' buy-in to not hiring the autorickshaws – as they were charging us double the metre amount to the bus stop and nearby *sabzi mandi*.

We have all agreed that we will try for a month or two, made pre-planned travel arrangements for the elderly people who cannot walk far, attributing to their knee problems, or school-going children for whom the weight of their books is too heavy to carry. I have noticed that some of the auto guys, who used to sit and read newspapers, did not even ask if we needed their service initially.

Gradually, every one of the 200 residents in our complex was trained not to glance at the auto guys. You know what? In one month, two guys vanished from our area. Two other guys are still adamant. But two of the elderly auto guys have begun asking us to consider their services. They have eventually agreed to ply on regular metre charges. Probably these guys stay close by and need some money – but who cares, we have won! Aditya's idea was simply brilliant. After the success with the auto guys, I have managed to introduce about thirty residents here to this Facebook community. All of them have been considering buying a home and all of them have signed up! And, of course, I am also happy to join this.'

This message had 3,800 *Likes* and over a thousand responses!

Aditya found a few messages from similar sceptics who had turned into believers now and hence joined the community.

If he needed a proof that his idea would work, this message was it. For anything to be called a *community*, it had to be driven by the community itself. If every message and its responses were to be provoked, Aditya would end up orchestrating an impossible act. If ever a community needed an anchor or a moderator to drive conversations, it would eventually fizzle out. The conversations in a community had to be this way – natural, unrestricted, and community-driven.

'Thank you in believing me. Today, all of you have believed in yourself. Thank you for listening to your inner conscience.

This is not my idea. It is everyone's idea. I am sure that every one of us thought about it at least once. But many of us might have resigned too early that forming a group, such as ours, is impossible. Buyers can unite and we have proved it. The power of our unity is not just a bargain, but a full-fledged war on Bengaluru's developers. At the rate that we are adding new people to this community, I will not be surprised if we hear about real estate price corrections in another six months. Let's sit tight!' answered Aditya to the last message. He then clicked on 'Like' associated with the original message.

He then posted a new message: 'I propose that we meet up this weekend to celebrate our growth. It would be a nice opportunity to know each one of you. May I propose a location on the Devanahalli road? We need to head out of Bengaluru city to accommodate 6715 people! ☺ Can we all gather behind the ITC factory on the Devanahalli road this Saturday at 11 a.m.?'

Within a minute of submitting his message, it was pouring responses, acceptances, and Likes. He was amazed that there were people online along with him and responded to him instantaneously.

When sceptics had turned believers, this community was all set to reach out to a new set of homebuyers and might multiply faster than anyone could believe.

That Saturday, Aditya managed to gather about 4,000 people behind the ITC factory. The rest of the folks did not join because of prior appointments and other weekend plans.

It was an incredible success story by any standard. Aditya reiterated that it was important to spread the message to only known contacts and serious homebuyers. The group agreed that this criterion of publicity alone could strengthen their purpose and make a difference in bringing down the prices of houses!

CHAPTER 12
THE PRESSURE POINT

M uting the CNBC channel in the presidential office room, Singhania joined the waiting team in the seating area.

It was Pritesh Singhania, Gaurav Singhania's nephew and the CEO of Singhania Energy Ltd., and a few members of his team who had scheduled a meeting that day.

Pritesh had a few issues, keeping him awake late into nights for the last few months. He had tried his best in bringing them early enough to Singhania who had his own thoughts on each of them. The suggested ways to resolve those issues had gone in a different tangent to what was expected. But things changed a lot, and to Pritesh, it was important to resolve them immediately.

Handing over a report, Pritesh finally said, 'Sir, here is a copy of the audit report which has been submitted to the government of India by CAI.' CAI was the Chief Auditor of India.

Singhania would not have noticed that a family member had to address him as 'sir'. But Pritesh was trained to address Singhania like that – just as anyone else was. Singhania had tried his best not to discriminate family members with other professionals joining the organisation, except for the not-so-vocally-spoken favour he had done – making Pritesh the CEO of Singhania Energy, the bread-and-butter business for the group.

Singhania had nurtured Pritesh for over ten years after he had completed his MBA at the Harvard University and joined the company. Only after Singhania had gained some confidence that Pritesh could run the core business for him, did he hand over the power seat and elevated himself to the chairman of Singhania Enterprises, the holding company of the group.

Adding his viewpoint on the CAI report, Pritesh said, 'CAI feels that we are not producing enough oil and gas for the nation. This report has emphasised that private, licensed players are bound by the contractual agreement in handling the national resources. We have to respond to a government's letter regarding this within the next ten days.'

'National resources? Who feels so? These are my resources. And I will produce enough when I see economics in it! Who will produce more oil when it is quoting at fifty dollars a barrel? And which business moron will produce more gas when all the prices are regulated? As if this is insufficient, I get dictated on whom to sell and at what price! Stupid fertiliser firms and other joker companies are the top priority. Why? Is it because the farmers need some cheap poison to consume and die!' responded Singhania.

Pritesh looked at three of his team members in the room: director of operations, director of technology and innovations, and manager of legal and company affairs. He then looked back at Singhania. Pritesh was sure that it was really not a response that Singhania wanted them to table for the government of India. He knew very well that many a time his uncle would slip into an unnecessary, self-indulging talk.

'Yes, we have been producing less oil and gas. And we will continue to do so! The oil and gas underneath my blocks will stay there for hundreds of years – whether we extract them today or not. We will produce more only when prices are completely deregulated and the government allows us to sell to whosoever gives better profits. Are we running a business or a charity foundation?' thundered Singhania.

Pritesh knew that he would soon get back to his normalcy. The transformation of his sentence construction – from using 'I' to 'we' – was the indication.

Singhania paused a while and walked away from the seating area and walked back. Continuing the discussion, he said, 'The government is only acting because there is an audit report in front of them. CAI *ne chabhi diya hai*. Don't I know that? Anyway, what do you suggest that we should do?' asked Singhania.

'Sir, one, we can request more time to send a response. Two, we can quote technical reasons for producing less crude oil and natural gas than expected,' said Pritesh.

'Good idea. Let's do that. I am sure we can produce realms of paper on complexity in deep-sea drilling and technical expertise required. This is an opportunity for us to slap CAI and wake them up. Let them know that drilling in deep sea is not like drilling a village well for water!'

The director of operations and the director of technology & innovations nodded in agreement.

It was certainly a good idea to use the pretext of technological challenges and justify the production levels in the offshore oil and gas exploration business. The deep-sea drilling would involve an intense study of geology and petrophysics of the locale, especially to understand rock formations, seismic profile, and geological pressure patterns undersea. Moreover, no oil and gas well could be drilled as a straight line. They could encounter unbreakable rocks when deviations in drilling would be required. What's more, there are a number of techniques like perforating a well in critical places to produce the right amount of pressure and extract the maximum amount of oil or gas output.

Singhania knew that they certainly had a big story to spin in the next ten days.

'So this matter is solved. What else makes you so worried that all of you turned up here?'

'Sir, there is another issue on hand,' said Pritesh. 'It is about Savita Offshore.'

Savita Offshore was a mid-sized offshore rigs provider in the country, with a fleet of six drill ships and a dozen offshore jack-up rigs. Drill ships and jack-up rigs are the essential tools used in oil and gas exploration business for deep-sea drilling. While jack-up rigs are the mobile platforms that could be towed to the location, drill ships offer even greater flexibility to move the rig from one location to another.

'What about Savita?' asked Singhania.

'Sir, they have been calling and pushing me to use their complete fleet.'

Singhania Energy had signed a contract with Savita for almost their entire fleet, except for two jack-up rigs and a drill ship. Singhania had used only half the contracted fleet so far – only because he was determined to produce less oil and gas. Instead, Singhania had lured Savita to take a retainer that paid them one-fifth of the market rates, just to keep them available and locked for Singhania Energy.

'Aren't we paying them the retainer that we have promised them on the unused fleet?'

'Yes, we are.'

Frowning heavily, Singhania shouted, 'Then what's the problem? They are getting ten lakhs a day for their idle assets! Everyone seems to demand the sun and the moon for what they have.'

'Sir, they have a huge debt on their balance sheet. And that is burning them for underutilised assets. Their point is that they could make five to six times that money if they are deployed somewhere else.'

Singhania was instantaneously provoked when he heard Pritesh say 'somewhere else'.

'Where will they deploy them? Who has motivation and money to drill when the crude oil prices have been under pressure?' thundered Singhania.

'I know for sure that there are dozens of drill ships and jack-up rigs that are idle today across the world, as we speak,' added Singhania sarcastically. 'They are just playing a trick with us to increase the retainer. I will not budge. The world is reeling under the pressure of a global slowdown, and it seems these are the only smart guys on the planet!'

'Shall I drop in our response to buy some more time?'

Singhania did not bother to hear what Pritesh had just said. He was still visibly irritated with the business pressure coming in from Savita Offshore. He said, 'The folks at Savita must be thinking that the government of India has sent a letter to increase the production and so we will come running to use the rest of their fleet.'

Pritesh knew the reality. It was not as if Savita Offshore had timed their business pressure now, coinciding with the government's pressure to increase the oil and gas production. Savita was genuinely expressing their concerns on mounting debt burden and inability to generate enough revenue from their assets for over several months now.

It was probably Pritesh's timing of bringing these two issues on the same day that had made Singhania think that they were synchronised events.

Pritesh would not mind in doubling the retainer for Savita on their unused assets. It was Singhania's idea to keep the tools ready but not use them until there was an emergency. In Pritesh's mind, the emergency was now. The government had begun to pressurise them in increasing the production. It was Singhania's arrogance that had put him in a block – in the past, and even now.

Pritesh also thought that perhaps he was wrong. He was too junior in this business. Singhania, on the other hand, had single-handedly run this business for a long time. What's more, Singhania was known for his shrewdness and business acumen that had powered exponential growth for the entire group.

Realising that Singhania paused for a while now, Pritesh asked, 'What do I do now?'

'Just buy some more time. We can neither be silly paying them anymore nor use the rigs right away. It is just not profitable for us!' Singhania gave his ultimatum.

CHAPTER 13
THE BIG QUAKE AND THE TIDAL WAVE

It was about 6.30 p.m. in Bengaluru, and Aditya saw an incoming call on his mobile. Pratap was trying to reach him.

'Hi, Pratap, what's up?'

'Are you watching the TV by any chance? A big earthquake struck Japan.'

'Is it? Let me check it out.'

Aditya cut the call and immediately switched on the TV. He then tuned into the BBC World.

The pictures of the earthquake began to unfold in front of his eyes, which gathered more information than what his ears could gather from the reporter's comments. The damage seemed limited, but the panic was clearly visible – some screamed in fear, some latched on to tables and immovable fixtures, and several others ran across the streets in panic. The visuals were a set of randomly gathered online videos, which were shot by locals on streets and office goers.

It was only after a few minutes of viewing the visuals that Aditya felt the shock for the first time, when he heard the reporter say, 'This is the biggest earthquake in the history of Japanese quakes – a 9.0 magnitude on the Richter scale.'

The facts then began to sink in Aditya's mind. The earthquake had hit the north-eastern coast of Japan near the city of Sendai in the Tōhoku region at 2.45 p.m. local time. The business damage reports began to pour; one of the prominent stories was that of a Nippon Oil Refinery, which had an accident. The thick black smoke, which filled an otherwise beautiful landscape around Sendai, began to emanate out of the refinery, indicating the severity of the earthquake. Robust buildings in nearby cities shook as if they we mere specimens in a town plan, but their determination to stand straight showed the advancement that the Japanese had attained in quake-proof civil engineering.

The damage was limited until a devastating tsunami had hit the Japanese north-east coast.

Aditya began to watch a delayed live visual of the tsunami on the TV.

The deep blue sea looked absolutely calm, even as shrieking birds flew away in fear. A set of small fishing boats, tied to the shore, floated over smooth-flowing ripples. The water level began to inch up as slowly as the sun would rise on the horizon. In less than three minutes, water began to gush towards the land. In the silence of deserted beach, the noise of gushing water eerily echoed in the circling winds, indicating an incoming disaster.

Water began to swell, and the waves began to pick up some momentum. Those small fishing boats began to rock – gently, initially and intensely, later. In less than a minute, the water level swelled to a considerable volume – so much so that the fishing boats were nudged out of their place, severing the links anchored to the shore. Slowly, but eventually, water began to gush on to the shore at a speed that could sow the seeds of fear. The momentum intensified so much that within a few seconds, numerous cars and vans parked onshore began to move along.

Then there were visuals of the aerial view of the sea that played on the TV.

A huge forthcoming wave, which ran across the coastline, gathered all the water it could as it travelled towards the shore. It was terrifying to watch that tsunami wave from those heights of flying helicopters. If one were to watch it from the ground level, it could kill people just by its sight! The insurmountable power of unforeseen size of tidal wave swept into the shore, taking whatever had come its way. And by the time it had reached the shore, it swelled to a 23-foot wall of water.

As some part of the waters smashed into the hilly rocks on the shore, the water bounced up into the sky some fifty feet.

Punching easily through an indestructible seawall, the rest of the 23-feet wall of water continued its juggernaut journey towards the civilised towns. It was a very scary and terrifying sight.

By now, the fishing boats were out of sight – they must have been crushed into unrecognisable litter by the weight of giant tide – and the mid-sized ferry boats, which looked like floating toys, came ashore. Gradually, large containers, from ships that had been capsized, began to swim to the shore in large numbers. The tsunami wave had carried those ships and the containers all the way from the deep sea, with an unimaginable ease, flaunting its destructive powers. Gathering all the black soil on the land, the terrifying, black wall of water continued its unstoppable journey. The containers crushed whatever else had come in their way – numerous houses, mansions, trees, cars, and bridges.

It was a devastating sight which mankind would never wish to see again.

The destruction, unfortunately, did not end there. This large tsunami wave reached almost ten kilometres inland, crushing anything and everything and strewing them all over the place. The containers crashed into the houses, the houses uprooted the trees, and the trees blew up the cars, and this horrifying domino effect continued for hours. The colossal loss of human life made the disaster even more terrible.

After two hours of uninterrupted watching and flipping to other news channels on the TV, Aditya was inundated with the news. He finally switched off the TV.

'Can you please join us here? We are all waiting for you,' said Meena. Aditya's mother and kids had also taken their seats for dinner.

Joining them for the dinner, Aditya said, 'What an unfortunate piece of land Japan is!'

Meena stared at him inquisitively.

Aditya added, 'I mean, look at the Japanese. They have managed to build a No. 3 economy in the world from such a tiny piece of land. Only disasters like this tell that they have been living on a shaky piece of land and it could jeopardise their nation building dreams.'

'Very true.'

'It's is very unfortunate that God has given them a land atop three tectonic plates. Anything can go wrong at any time. The power of nature can override their determination to remain an economic powerhouse.'

The next morning, Aditya woke up to the confirmed news of a failed nuclear cooling system. The previous night, the nuclear power plant had been reported to be in trouble.

A cooling system was supposed to have switched on automatically when the production was stalled abruptly. The massive earthquake, however, had failed one of the cooling systems, pushing the plant into a likely meltdown scenario. The news analysts on the TV were a worried lot: If a meltdown were to happen, the reactors would get heated up, spreading dangerous radioactive substances into the environment.

After several hours of futile cooling efforts using sea water, one of the six nuclear reactors at the damaged power plant began to crumble. What followed began to confirm the worst fear – the number of rescue workers was reduced or nearly evacuated from the site. And within the next couple of hours, the first reactor exploded, an explosion which was dramatic and breathtakingly captured live by the TV cameras.

After the first nuclear reactor explosion, the power plant witnessed a cascading and vicious loop of ever-increasing radiation and failing cooling systems. The next day, one more reactor exploded. And then it was clear that the other reactors would also give-in with the passing time. Unfortunately, the nuclear reactors exploded one after the other as though they were configured as serial bomb blasts.

After one complete week of watching the triple disaster that had struck Japan, Aditya did some more research. The Japanese nuclear disaster was one of the worst such incidents in the world – the last complete meltdown had taken place at Chernobyl in Ukraine.

When Aditya saw the pictures of disaster site and its vicinity in Chernobyl, he could not imagine the scale of damage. The neighbouring towns of Chernobyl were deserted for over the last two decades.

Seeing those scary pictures, the first question that came to his mind was what will happen if such a nuclear disaster were to happen in India. Will the Indian administration be able to respond to it like the Japanese had managed?

The next question that came to his mind was what if such a disaster could really happen in India. When he googled for some analysis on Indian tectonic plate and seismic risks, he could not believe the stunning facts: Silluru in Andhra Pradesh and Shindra in Gujarat were in seismic risk zones 3 and 4, making them very risky. Both of these power plants had been under construction. Another nuclear power plant planned near Kone village, along the western coastline in Karnataka, was also in seismic risk zone 4.

Aditya had trouble sleeping that night. He was unable to erase the visuals of the Japanese tsunami, nuclear disaster, Chernobyl's deserted villages, and his research findings that three of the upcoming nuclear power plants in India were at risk. And among those haunting pictures emerged a vivid image of what he could do next.

Maybe the planets had conspired in letting Aditya take his war on Singhania to the next level. But he certainly had a plan now. Indeed a big plan! And he knew an important person who could help him in realising this.

CHAPTER 14
THE LAUNCH OF GAME-CHANGING TOWNSHIP

Vivek and his team were in the boardroom, undergoing the usual tension that they experienced every quarter. This time, Singhania had defined a single-point agenda for the discussion – that is around the launch of a game-changing township. In the previous three months, Vivek and his team had worked on no other project but this one.

Moving the entire machinery, Vivek had conducted an exhaustive feasibility study and prepared a mega plan – to transform an 85-acre land near BEL circle into a land of dream destination for thousands of homebuyers in Bengaluru. As part of the feasibility study, Vivek had found that the market was not ready for an ultra-luxury villa project at Whitefield, but there was a pent-up demand for budget-apartments. Owing to the current slowdown in the economy, Singhania was also convinced that the township project would be the best priority. Vivek had sailed through the township proposal, when the team presented two of their selling propositions – one, the vicinity of project to the proposed Bengaluru Metro Railway line; two, with the world-class infrastructure inside the township, the sales of budget apartments were expected to be overwhelming.

Switching off the CNBC channel in the presidential office room and joining the waiting team in the boardroom, Singhania said, 'Good morning, boys.'

'Good morning, sir.' The team rose from their seats and sat down after greeting him.

'Let me see the plan. I cannot wait any more,' said Singhania without wasting any time.

Satish spread the blueprint on the huge, mahogany red centre table. The first blueprint had a customer-friendly illustration, a bird's-eye view of the project. This blueprint showed a number of apartment blocks and the layout of all amenities. The Outer Ring Road was seen running on the west side of the project and a 100-feet main road on its east side.

'Sir, we have adopted a butterfly design for our township,' said Vivek. Pointing towards the two big green parks and building blocks around it, he added, 'This will come out very grand – something that the city has never seen before.'

Pointing to the centre of the blueprint, Vivek then said, 'This is where we have planned for a beautiful and massive fountain. We have planned for an amphitheatre as the butterfly's head and a curved, clubhouse with a swimming pool positioned at the other end – at its tail. The clubhouse will have all indoor games – snooker, table tennis, caroms, gymnasium, library, and a multipurpose party hall. Adjacent to the swimming pool, this section of the clubhouse will have a Jacuzzi and sauna for ladies and gents, separately.'

Vivek's finger stopped at the clubhouse on the blueprint as he heard Singhania speak.

'I really like this,' said Singhania. 'The amphitheatre as the butterfly head and clubhouse at its tail is an excellent idea. It looks super impressive. Good job, guys!'

Singhania had a spark in his eyes, which the team had never seen. He was clearly delighted.

Moving his finger again on the blueprint and pointing towards the amenities marked out in a green area, which was shaped as butterfly wings, Vivek said, 'On this right wing, we have planned for kids' play area. It would have a skating ring and a few toddlers' play gear. On this left wing, we have planned for a tennis court and a basketball court for men and women.'

'It looks good.'

'We will have eight towers along each of the wings. So, totally, sixteen residential blocks will come up along the perimeter of the wings,' said Vivek.

Pointing to a mall in the blueprint, Vivek added, 'We have planned for this 3,00,000 square feet commercial mall that houses about seventy-five large-sized retail outlets and restaurants over three floors. Our team has finalised the contract with PVR cinemas for a multiplex on the top floor. PVR has come back to us with a plan for twelve screens and a bowling alley.'

In the blueprint, the commercial mall was located in the south-west corner of the township project that had access from the Outer Ring Road, making it easy to create an entry to the general public as well as to the residents of the township.

Vivek then guided Singhania towards the second set of the blueprints, which had the front and side elevation illustrations. Each of the residential blocks had eighteen floors.

'With eighteen floors each, the towers will look stunning. By spreading them evenly around the butterfly wings, they will also appear neat and not like crowded concrete jungle,' said Vivek.

Pointing to the night view of the skyline, he added, 'Look at this, sir. The night sky in Bengaluru would get a stunning makeover.' The artist's illustration of night views of fully lit apartment blocks was really impressive as if a thousand lighthouses would come together in the township. In comparison, the day-view illustration of the apartment blocks looked pale, even though it depicted a rich surface of unpolished granite and a good blend of white, ivory, and dark brown mosaic of paints.

Jumping and chuckling like a child, Singhania pounced on to the front elevation illustration and said, 'Hey, look at this clubhouse. It looks like a Lilliput in front of the residential towers.' He was clearly taking pride in those fully lit, massive residential blocks.

It was a long time since Vivek and his team had seen Singhania this excited. He was only known for his arrogance and grumpy, stern face. They were all really happy that their big boss liked what they had painstakingly planned and architected. If all the projects that they had worked so far were at one level, this township project was indeed a very daunting one. It had tested the meat of every guy on the team – working with the architects, engineers, and creative agencies was never so difficult. For the pressure of delivering the marketing collaterals and making this presentation that day, Vivek himself had to do three night-outs at the creative agency's office – working along creative folks round-the-clock on Adobe Illustrator and Photoshop, eating office-delivered Domino's pizza and Coke, and taking short naps on the couch. The rest of his team had to undergo this routine on countless design iterations for more than ten days.

'Guys, I am super impressed with the plan. It is high time that we get this rolling in the market. Bengaluru will sit up and take notice! Just tell me how much you need to launch this immediately,' said Singhania.

Looking at the director of finance, Vivek said, '250 crores?'

'Yes, sir, 250 crores,' said the finance guy.

'What's our cash position?'

'Sir, we can do this only if we pledge more shares. But we have already pledged 65 per cent of our stake.'

Turning to Vivek, Singhania said, '65 per cent is nothing. You can pledge more. Do a high-decibel advertising campaign in the *Times of India*, let the share price go up a little, and then pledge another 20 per cent! I want this out immediately.'

Jumping on the opportunity, Vivek said, 'Sure, sir.'

CHAPTER 15
SOWING THE SEEDS OF FEAR

Aditya felt at home in Prof. Srinivas's residence which reflected the simplicity of a teacher in every visible thing in the room – a cane-made sofa set, with its cushions draped in pure cotton, flaunting an elegant applique work; a glass-topped cane centre-table which matched with the rest of the furniture; a small but intricately designed jute carpet, stretching from the edge of the sofa to underneath the centre table and adding a lot of comfort to the feet. With no TV in the room and minimal wall décor, consisting of mostly etched teak murals, the focus of the living room was maintained on the large bookshelf. The range of topics the books covered indicated the intellectual quotient of the man that he had been sitting with.

Srinivas, dressed in simple white *kurta* and *pyjama*, leisurely sat in front of Aditya, listening.

Aditya briefed Srinivas on his research findings on Chernobyl and the Indian nuclear plants' vulnerability.

Responding to Aditya, Srinivas said, 'It is terrible to note that three of the upcoming nuclear power plants are in seismic risk zone 3 and above. But what do you plan to do with it?' Srinivas was still clueless on why Aditya had to travel all the way from Bengaluru to share this piece of information.

'Let me ask you this – what will you do if I say that your house is haunted?'

'What?'

'Just a hypothetical question – what will you do?'

'Should I be worried? I don't know. I have never seen such a thing at my home.'

'Fine, what if I demonstrate it for you? Would you believe?'

Prof. Srinivas had no clue of what Aditya was talking about. Looking at his blood-red eyes, dark circles underneath, and unkempt hair, Srinivas was unsure if he needed medical attention for all his apparent sleepless routine.

He was unwilling to respond, yet Srinivas gave Aditya's hypothetical question some thinking and responded, 'If I see facts in your demonstration, I will be really worried. It is scary to think that my house has been haunted.'

Aditya got the answer that he was looking for.

'Great!' exclaimed Aditya. 'That is exactly what I had in mind for the last two days.'

Srinivas just stared at him in a daze. He had more than one question that he wanted to ask Aditya.

'Wait, let me explain,' said Aditya as if he had read the confusion in Srinivas's mind. 'The villagers of Silluru are no different from the villagers in the Tōhoku region of Japan. The Japanese in Tōhoku and Miyagi prefecture are being evacuated from their residences, as we speak – some hundreds of kilometres away from their homes, which they had carefully built. And dumping back all the farms that they had grown every day, they are now queuing up for a bowl of soup and noodles in rescue camps.'

Srinivas stopped thinking of everything else and began to listen to Aditya raptly. It was clear that Aditya needed no medical attention – Aditya clearly had something that needed his attention now.

Aditya added, 'Just imagine – what would be going on in the minds of those thousands of Japanese now? Uncertainty of what's in store for them. Fear of losing everything they had until now. What will the villagers of Silluru do, if they were to know that they might lose their homes and farms one day?'

It was crystal clear on what Aditya had in mind. And Srinivas could see that Aditya had his eyes set on Singhania, who had a huge stake in getting Silluru Nuclear Power Plant ready and commissioned as soon as possible.

Srinivas recollected the day when Pratap had called him to inform how Aditya had lost his business to Singhania's arrogant business dreams. He could only imagine the pain that Aditya had gone through that day. He was not even by Aditya's side to console him. Today, Aditya was right across the table with an idea that aimed at terrorising his enemy. He would be very happy to support Aditya.

Looking straight into Aditya's eyes and extending his moral strength, Srinivas said, 'I got you! How can I help you?'

'I need a seminar,' said Aditya. 'A seminar on the danger to the Indian nuclear power plants from earthquakes – from an expert whom the people of Silluru would believe, from an expert who can illustrate the dangers of living by a nuclear power plant which could crack any moment, from an expert who can sow the seeds of fear!'

Srinivas was stunned to hear that. Aditya's blood-red eyes, which he had thought were the result of a sleepless night, were discernibly burning with an indestructible desire to win the war that Aditya had chosen to fight.

Yes, Aditya was an opportunistic. For an unfair deal that Singhania had offered, Aditya deserved an overwhelming support. It was clear that a good businessman would remain a businessman at heart – opportunistic, selfish, and intense. In a tragedy that the entire world had been reeling under, Aditya had selfishly scouted an opportunity. But how would it matter? Didn't someone say all was fair in love and war?

In the war against the arrogant, mighty Singhania, Aditya needed his support that day. And Srinivas was glad to offer it.

'I have a friend who is an expert on geophysics and teaches along with me. If what you found is right, he might resonate with a need to educate the villagers on the lurking potential danger.'

Pulling out a zoomed-in map of Andhra Pradesh on his laptop, Aditya pointed to the area around Sriharikota. To the north of Sriharikota, along the edge of the Bay of Bengal, Srinivas could find a small dot named Silluru. It was flanked by a few villages: Haralooru, Parvatipuram, Gopannapalli, Sripuram, Rayudupalli, Ramavaram, Venkannapalem, Yeleswaram, Krishnudupalem, and Palamooru.

Aditya said, 'There are about a dozen villages around Silluru. I just want us to focus on conducting informal seminars – be it under the banyan trees or inside the residences of influential villagers. But we should focus only on these dozen villages.' Aditya then added, 'I also think we have to reach out to an NGO around Silluru. Only an NGO-approach will make this story credible.'

Srinivas said, 'Yes, that's a very good idea. I can do that too.'

Hailing from the state of Andhra Pradesh, it would be far easier for Prof. Srinivas to connect with the people in native language than it would be for Aditya. And Srinivas's credibility as a professor from India's premier institution would help in believing the need to educate the locals on a lurking danger.

'Thank you. Thanks a lot!'

If everything were to go as planned, the seeds of fear would soon be sowed – at Silluru – in the interiors of Andhra Pradesh.

CHAPTER 16
Just a Pinch

Singhania looked worried with a copy of the unaudited quarterly results in front of him. Flipping the sheets, repeatedly from front to back, he stared at the mocking numbers which were tabulated. This was a set of numbers which had no correlation with the previous quarters' profit-and-loss data. He had not seen such out of place numbers in his entire entrepreneurial journey.

Is this a joke? Singhania thought. He turned red with anger. Nobody in the world could dare to play a prank with him.

On one hand, he was irritated with the sales performance at the just-launched township project, and on the other hand, he was shocked with the outrageous sales from the eight projects at Koramangala, Nagarabhavi, Sarjapur Road, JP Nagar 8th Phase, and Old Madras Road.

Or is there any discrepancy? Singhania had another thought. The frown on his face began to grow bigger. Nobody in the world could share such a discrepancy with Singhania without verification.

Either way, feeling an immediate need to discuss and understand from Vivek, Singhania picked up his mobile and dialled a number.

'Good afternoon, sir,' answered Vivek calmly, but hesitantly.

'What the heck is this, Vivek?'

Vivek knew what Singhania was coming to. It was less than half an hour since he had sent the quarterly report. The accounted revenue and the order book was certainly a worry.

Realising that Vivek was silent at the other end, Singhania added, 'Is there any discrepancy in this data? Or is the order book so pathetic in Bengaluru?'

'The data is correct, sir. I verified it before sending it. The order book is indeed very bad.'

'I just don't understand this. The last quarterly results were fine. But I cannot understand what has suddenly gone so bad there. What do you think our investors will do with this kind of numbers?'

Vivek chose not to answer this question. Singhania surely had a point here.

Singhania frustratingly added, 'Take a look at the notes to the sales data, once again, Vivek. You have managed to get bookings for two flats at the Sarjapur Road project, one flat at JP Nagar, one flat at Koramangala, three in Nagarabhavi, four flats at our newly launched township project . . . This is not just *pathetic*. It is indeed *shocking*!'

Singhania's voice had almost punched a hole in his eardrum.

'Sir, probably the economic slowdown is showing up. There has been a remarkable change in the number of customers visiting the project sites. Three to four months ago, we had very good footfall over the weekends. These days, the project sites are deserted over the weekdays and sparsely visited over the weekends.'

Sticking to his point, Singhania asked, 'Do you think we can go with this set of numbers to the street? Our investors are going to dump us, damn it!'

Singhania was correct. The unaudited results had indicated a steep 86 per cent drop in the net profit for the quarter! The share price would also nosedive, just as their net profit did.

'Sir, I will investigate this slump in our numbers further and take corrective actions.'

Singhania got infuriated with the first few words coming from Vivek. 'What did you say? You *will* investigate? Are you admitting that you have no clue as to what's happening there?'

'Sir, our energies were completely focused on the township project, which we all decided to put on a superfast track.'

'Are you trying to put the blame on me, then?'

'No, sir. Absolutely not. The team has really put in a lot of effort in launching the township project.'

'Well, I did appreciate your work on the township project, didn't I?' asked Singhania. 'But you cannot take that as an excuse for this non-performance! In any case, what great job did you and your boys do after the launch of township? Are you saying that you have shaken the earth and the heaven by selling *four flats?*'

With Singhania's voice drilling through his ear, Vivek had a hard time holding on to his BlackBerry at the ear. Not knowing what to say now, he just filled the pause with an 'Hmm . . .'

'I don't know what you will do in the next one month. I need to see a good order book or else you'd better search for another job!'

Singhania did not even wait for an answer. He cut the call immediately.

In a daze, Vivek walked towards the huge glass window showing the Bengaluru skyline and the busy roads below, as seen from his tenth-floor office on MG Road. The streets had the same buzz as ever – people were busy driving and honking on the way to their offices and to the shopping centres. The Food World store, which was visible from his office on one side, was as crowded as it always would be at this hour of the day. The Bangalore Central, whose food courts were visible from his office on the other side, also had the same volume of everyday lunchtime crowd.

Vivek began to think.

Thinking intensely, he asked himself, *What's going on with the real estate in Bengaluru? Are people spending on essential grocery and food but not on discretionary real estate? But spending on food in restaurants is also considered discretionary. If there is indeed a slowdown in India, where are these people coming from – driving all the way to MG Road to shop and eat? Singhania is probably right. Selling eleven flats in a quarter is inexplicable. But am I alone in experiencing this? How are the other developers doing?*

Vivek was still thinking: *Are there any serious deficiencies with my team? But they were extremely busy with the launch of the township project until the last month. Probably all the energies went in for the township project in the last three months! But still how can sales slip through the cracks?'*

In his career of twenty-five-plus years, these were certainly testing times. His credibility was at stake. What's more, Vivek felt jittery with Singhania's phrases – *non-performance,* a sarcastic one on *earth-and-heaven shaking,* and a direct reference to *search for another job.*

Turning back, walking towards his cabin door, and opening it a little, Vivek asked his secretary, 'Can you please ask Satish to join me for a discussion immediately?'

Vivek needed a detailed investigation on what had gone wrong in the last three months. He wanted to put a concrete plan and increase the sales immediately.

PART IV

THE DELUGE

CHAPTER 17
THE NETWORK EFFECT

Aditya had been working with Prof. Srinivas on arranging seminars in over a dozen villages around Silluru. The geophysics professor at the IIT had confirmed his research findings and had agreed for giving the required talk. Srinivas had also made a significant progress on roping in an NGO, as per the plan.

While Aditya was still in Chennai, one day he noticed an incoming call from Kannan.

'Hi, Kannan, how are you doing?'

'Great, sir!'

'How are things in Bengaluru?'

'Bengaluru? Are you not in Bengaluru now?'

'No, I am in Chennai with Prof. Srinivas. The war on Singhania is entering its second phase now!' Aditya laughed out loud.

'Great, sir. And I have some information to share on the first phase of your war,' said Kannan, chuckling.

'What's that?'

'Singhania has pledged an additional 20 per cent of his stake in Singhania Realty with us very recently. He wanted it to fund his dream project – the newly launched township project at BEL circle. Right now, he has pledged about 85 per cent of his stake. I don't know if you have noticed the high-decibel advertising. Singhania had bought the complete edition of the *Property Times* and the *Times of India*. Every page carried his advertisement for the township project!'

'OK?' Aditya's eyes began to bulge out as he keenly heard Kannan.

'But I get to understand that the sales were pathetic. Singhania and his team have managed to sell just four flats in the township project!'

'How do you know?'

'Sir, Indian National Bank is the only bank to get customer details for any loan processing. This was the deal that our guys managed to negotiate with Vivek at the time of funding through pledged shares. I also understand that we have negotiated that our bank should have this advantage for the first three months of the launch!'

Aditya jumped with excitement and said, 'Excellent piece of information!'

'Did you get to see the action in the Facebook community of late?'

Wondering why Kannan suddenly changed the topic, Aditya curiously asked, 'No, why?'

'When I came to know about the pathetic apartment sales at Singhania's township project from my colleague, I checked the Facebook community page last night – just out of curiosity.'

'OK?'

'There are 53,912 members as of last night.'

'What?'

'Ya, didn't you check it of late?'

'No. I am glued on to something else that is important. But this is amazing – 53,912 members?' Aditya screamed happily in all his excitement.

What was driving that membership at the Facebook community was 'the network effect'. While Aditya initially created the Facebook update and shared an email with only 200 of his contacts, by the time it had reached the contacts of his contacts, it was another story. He had 6,715 members in the 2nd degree of the network effect. By now, many unknown contacts of the contacts of his contacts had become a member. This growth would only compound with the 3rd, 4th, and 5th degrees of the network!

'Sir, you would not imagine what you have created on the Facebook. I did go through some of the updates. People are taking immense pride in rejecting the calls from the real estate sales guys. While rejecting the offers, one guy apparently said,

"Apartment? With the prices so sky-high, you better go to the moon and sell there". Another guy apparently said, "FREE *mein milega*? Sorry, I am not interested in any apartment!" There are hundreds of such posts, and I see thousands of people enjoying the conversations, laughing and rolling on the floor as per their updates and *Likes*!'

Aditya was simply overwhelmed with these inputs.

Kannan continued, 'Sir, you will win this war. Here is an opportunity to pinch Singhania a little more. Can you go short on his shares? The quarterly results of Singhania Realty are due in a week.'

Going short on shares was a trading technique to sell the shares first and buy them later. This technique would be used if one was confident that the share price would go down. Here was Kannan who had indirect information that the quarterly sales might be very bad.

'Go short? Are you sure?'

Kannan still could not forget the day when he had watched Aditya kneeling on the ground and collapsing in front of the factory. Singhania had taken away everything from his life and threw a few rupees change as if Aditya was a beggar. The war that Aditya had resolved to wage against the mighty Singhania was the war of his life. This was no ordinary business war.

'Sir, I know this is not a game. This is your life and your war against an arrogant businessman. I cannot afford to suggest anything that might put you in trouble.' Kannan's voice was deep, confident, and empathetic.

'Thank you. I always appreciate your help. I will bet a small amount. How about one crore for going short?'

'I feel you should increase your bet.'

'How much would you bet if you were in my place?'

'Twelve crores?'

'Wouldn't that be too much? That is almost everything of what I have managed to get from Singhania. What if we go wrong?'

'Believe me, the market will be as shocked as you and I are, if Singhania Realty posts a bad set of numbers. And as per my information, the probability of that event happening is too high. And in my opinion, the risk reward is in favour of betting big on negative news that the market is least prepared for. After all, you have orchestrated this with great care!'

Kannan's points were very valid. His financial and brokerage experience was up for grabs.

'You are making sense. But for me to bet that big, I need a little time to think. By the way, Shaji supplies to Singhania Realty. Maybe I should check with him on how Renuka Steel's stock is moving to Singhania's projects?'

'You can . . . but . . .' Kannan dragged his words uncomfortably.

'But what?'

'You need to discount the stock that Singhania would have lifted for his township project. We have disbursed 250 crores for his pledged shares – almost the entire amount was for buying truckloads of steel, jelly, sand, and cement. Three months of raw material supply to be precise.'

'I see your point. You are great. But let me get some insights from Shaji too and then let us plan the next operation.'

'Operation Crush!' said Kannan, liberally giving it a fancy title, and then chuckled.

'Operation Crush. Nice one!' yelled Aditya with a loud laughter.

CHAPTER 18
THE BIG CRASH AND THE BIG CASH

S inghania never thought he would see a day like this. He was watching the CNBC channel as the anchors began quizzing Vivek Mathur live, on-air, through a telephonic conversation.

The audited quarterly and annual results were shared with the media that morning. Singhania Realty had reported a drop of 80 per cent in its sales and 84 per cent in its net profit. The share price crashed 32 per cent, and it was just two minutes since the trading had begun that morning.

'Mr Mathur, we have seen a couple of real estate companies which announced their quarterly results earlier this week. While there is a pinch in their net profits, what explains a massive 84 per cent drop in your net profit?' asked the anchor.

'There is a clear indication that the homebuyers are not actively buying these days. With the visible slowdown in India and recessionary conditions across the world, the buyers seem to postpone their decisions.'

The anchor persisted and asked again, 'But a massive drop of 84 per cent in your net profit seems unfathomable!'

'You should note that Singhania Realty is only focused on Bengaluru market. Today, we command over 20 per cent market share – that is if you consider all the organised segment of the projects in the city. The IT sector is going through uncertain times, owing to the global financial meltdown. Obviously, the spending of IT executives in Bengaluru, a concentrated city with these professionals, has suffered. We are, very frankly, feeling the pinch for our concentration on a single city for growth.'

Vivek had uncomfortably recollected this rehearsed response to an expected question in his office. The entire team had anticipated a list of questions and drafted a convincing response for each of them. Vivek had sought prior permission from Singhania on the team's suggested responses.

Watching the live conversation on the TV, Singhania said to himself, 'Concentration of growth in a single city? Look at who is talking? The guy does not even know how to sell!'

In the meantime, Singhania's eyes rolled over the TV screen in search for the ticker. The share price of Singhania Realty was now down by 35 per cent!

'You stupid, your talk is only accelerating the fall! Stop this nonsense!' Singhania madly shouted in his cabin – all alone.

'Mr Mathur, how do you plan to overcome this situation? What is your guidance for the next quarter?' asked another anchor on the TV.

Singhania switched off the TV immediately in frustration. He knew what Vivek would be telling them. It was all rehearsed for over the last twenty-four hours in the office. Vivek's words had so far only accentuated the fall of the share price, and Singhania was least interested to hear the rehearsed storyline any more.

Throwing his hands up into the air intermittently and cursing Vivek all along, he walked furiously from one end of the cabin to another. He walked at thrice his normal speed now.

The next day, the market started beating the share price again. It opened 13 per cent lower to the previous day's closing price.

Singhania was totally upset over that investor reaction to the worst quarterly performance ever. He picked up the phone to place a call.

The moment it was picked up, he said, 'Vivek, please call up Indian National Bank and find out what's happening in the market. We cannot sit idle with 85 per cent of our stake pledged with them. The market is hammering our share price!'

'Sir, I am already on call with those folks on the other line. I will call you back with an update very soon.'

Singhania disconnected the call. Pale faced, he looked very concerned.

This pledging of shares could turn out very nasty, sometimes. People lose their business to bankers for leveraging their balance sheets relentlessly. Singhania would be the last person on this earth to lose his real estate business, for what seemed to be a silly short-term pain.

***

Picking up the incoming call from Kannan, Aditya asked, 'What's up?'

'Sir, did you square off your position?'

Aditya had short-sold Singhania Realty shares three days before the announcement of quarterly results. He had a discussion with Shaji on steel supplies to Singhania's projects. But he went with Kannan's judgement on the market information and sold Singhania Realty shares with an intention to buy them low – very low, indeed!

'No, not so far.'

'Sir, we have made a killing. The stock has got hammered over 50 per cent from our price. Please square off the position – now!' Kannan almost commanded when he said 'now'.

Aditya recollected the big flat-screen TV that played CNBC TV-18 when he was inside Singhania's palatial office room. He imagined what pain Singhania might be going through, right now, watching his stock crash like mad!

'Singhania's 84 per cent drop in net profit is too tempting. I think I should hold on to the position for some more time. The market is running havoc on his real estate business. I wish he is watching the TV right now and feeling the pain!'

'Sir, I am sorry, but this is not the time to indulge in unnecessary emotions. Our guys have received a call from Vivek's office here. The directive now from the top guy of our bank is to buy the shares from the open market and support the price!'

'Goodness gracious. Thank you. I will square off the position now,' said Aditya. 'Just hold.'

He clicked a few buttons on the trading website and then paused for a minute. 'Thank you. I am done. We have just managed to grow our twelve crores to seventy-five crores!' Aditya cried out in excitement.

'Great. Singhania's big crash and your big cash!' Kannan laughed out loud.

'Thank you for making this happen. Our corpus to bring down Singhania's empire has just got bigger,' said Aditya and burst out into laughter.

Aditya felt invincible at that moment!

CHAPTER 19
PERSISTENCE!

Aditya logged on to the Facebook community after a week. Within a week, the members at The Real Estate Brigade had swollen to 73,000+. The strength of this army was building up amazingly by each passing day.

Aditya updated the Facebook Wall. 'Friends, I am very impressed with the way we are building our strength every day. 73,000 homebuyers within Bengaluru are solid enough to piss off the developers! Btw, did any one of you follow the stock markets? You would have noticed that many developers focused on Bengaluru have reported dismal quarterly numbers. Net profits dipped anywhere between 65 to 85 per cent. This is our success so far. I will not be surprised to see developers throwing at us irresistible offers very soon. Please resist your temptations in giving into them. I am sure that 40 per cent discount that we are all aiming for is not too far away! With your permission, may I change the rule #3 to: Please BANG as you hang up the phone, when you hear a call from any real estate developer from now on? Please intensify your campaign and let more of your friends, who are looking forward to buying a home, embrace this community. There are still some folks who are buying a few houses out there. We need to stop that!'

That was it. That was all that Aditya wanted the brigade of 73,000+ soldiers to do from then on. He had hit upon a basic human emotion of greed. He used those few words to add more appetisers to the already greedy homebuyers.

His modification of Rule #3 was a masterstroke of his business acumen. He knew that people generally fall for offers, but if he could find a way for people to stop listening to offers, he would win. What better way than to just simply hang up on the phone!

Aditya added, 'Btw, folks, please check this link from the *Times of India*. Get greedy, folks!' He pasted the link. The title of the news report said, 'Postpone buying a home. Prices to drop by 20 per cent in Bengaluru.'

The media began to cover a hot new story in those days. The media's selling of this story of greed was an indication that the real estate price correction had just begun.

Folding his hands behind his back, Vivek walked across the large hall in his office. An army of telecallers sat along the entire length of a wall. They were all trained to propose an attractive offer and get an appointment with homebuyers.

Vivek began to eagerly listen to the callers while they were busy calling. Each of the telecaller had a headset – a set of speakers and a microphone to make a soft sales pitch.

'Sir, this is Bhargavi calling from Singhania Realty . . .'

The first call was disappointing. Bhargavi turned around and looked at Vivek and Satish. Her expression stated that the person had not even given her a chance to speak.

'That's OK. Please call the next person,' said Satish.

'Sir, this is Bhargavi calling from Singhania Realty . . .' She placed the next call.

Another call, same fate. This time, she did not turn around. She knew what the expectation would be. Looking into the Excel file provided by the company, she picked up the next number and placed another call.

'Sir, this is Bhargavi calling from Singhania Realty . . .' Same response. She was not even getting a chance to say the next few words.

Vivek and his team had designed an irresistible offer: 'Pay 20 per cent now and the rest at the time of occupation.'

Singhania Realty was sitting pretty on a huge, unsold inventory of 2,500 flats across Bengaluru. Except for the flats in the township project, many of them were over 75 per cent complete. So, even if they could get a buyer pay 20 per cent upfront, the balance would only be due within the next five to six months.

Nevertheless, the offer could sound irresistible for any homebuyer – if, and only if, they were prepared to hear it over the phone.

Bhargavi placed over twenty calls in the next fifteen minutes. She worked at her job with a clockwork precision, just as trained. She looked for a number, placed the call through the system, waited for the dialling tone and the respondent's voice, and then began to read from the pitch document. Each call placed consumed less than a minute before a user answered.

Bhargavi's success of getting through a potential homebuyer after twenty calls was zero!

Overhearing the callers, Vivek frantically walked up and down the room. Bhargavi, Kavita, Priya, Sweta, Kajal, and other girls made several calls. They all had voices that were sexy enough for men to listen to. But Vivek was bewildered at how callously the homebuyers hung up.

The calling operation in that room resembled a battlefield. The brigade of twelve telecallers was religiously calling as if they were shooting non-stop from their bunkers. And behind them were Vivek and Satish, who looked like an army colonel and his lieutenant, encouraging and ordering what to do next.

After nearly an hour of intense calling, the overall success rate of this brigade of telecallers was zero. That was zero success rate achieved after firing nearly thousand bullets!

'What the hell is going on in Bengaluru?' asked Vivek. 'Are we selling some credit card or personal loans? Why are these people not even listening to an offer that we are trying to make?'

Satish stared at him. He too had no clue on what was happening. He just shrugged his shoulders in confusion.

CHAPTER 20

SIX FEET IN THE LAND OF SILLURU

In the interiors of Andhra Pradesh and in the land of Silluru, a set of six feet of three new soldiers had been marching. They were marching every inch of this area, brainwashing every villager that they had come across and instilling fear that had only begun to grow.

The three new soldiers who got added to Aditya's camp were Prof. Srinivas, Prof. Balasubramaniam, and Venkateswarlu. Balasubramaniam was the IIT professor who confirmed Aditya's nuclear vulnerability findings, and Venkateswarlu was the head of a wide-network NGO in the vicinity of Silluru.

The trio had managed to visit eleven villages in the vicinity of Silluru.

That day was the final day of their ten-day camp – the last village on their itinerary. They had managed to get a group of 350 villagers under a banyan tree which had a raised cement platform around it. While the trio sat on the platform, the villagers had squatted on the mother earth.

The trio played a few videos that were downloaded from YouTube – the terrifying videos of the Japanese tsunami, nuclear disaster, and rescue operations. When those disaster videos played on a giant white screen under the shade of the big banyan tree, they captivated the entire village. Some held their hands together in fear, some closed their eyes with their hands as the horror videos played, a few ladies nervously played with their *saree pallus*, and many others just stared without batting an eyelid. This was a similar scene in all the surrounding villages around Silluru.

'Are you sure that I have to lose my farm in a likely nuclear disaster?' asked an old man when the team finished their briefing and showing them the videos. The question could not be more naive than that.

'If the air that you breathe is intoxicated, where is the point in staying back and farming your land? You will be relocated if such a disaster were to strike us,' answered Venkateswarlu.

'Relocated? Where?' asked the old man, looking at the men around him.

'That depends on the extent of the damage. In a similar incident at Chernobyl, people had to be relocated hundreds of kilometres away. The nuclear disaster that happened there was at the highest level – a complete nuclear meltdown with the highest level of radiation,' said Prof. Balasubramaniam.

'Cher . . . Where?'

'Chernobyl. It is in Ukraine, once a part of Russia.'

The word Russia seemed to ring a bell. The old man nodded his head gently. The facts sunk in slowly into his head, but his eyes dreadfully probed for something else.

'If I were to get compensated for potential losses, I am fine,' said another villager.

'It is fine if you get compensated by the government or the companies that run the nuclear plants. But maybe you should know that the victims of Bhopal gas tragedy are still waiting for the compensation that the company had promised them to. And it is already over twenty-five years!' answered Venkateswarlu.

The villager had a frustrating frown on his face and began to look at other villagers around him in disbelief. He was clearly taken aback by the snub, probably least prepared to hear such a fact.

'Yes, I read that in the newspapers,' said a young villager from the crowd. He wore a regular striped shirt and pants. He appeared a little educated and college-going.

'Did you . . . ?' asked a few villagers around him, spontaneously.

Looking at them and confirming their fear, the young man said, 'Yes, I read that.'

'If a gas tragedy in India could kill thousands, imagine what a nuclear disaster could do. Nuclear disasters do not differentiate between humans, animals, or plants. It will kill all of us in the nick of time. The air gets polluted faster than our imagination. The soil turns toxic for several decades. Even if you are fortunately alive,' said Prof. Srinivas, 'you will find it tough to live. You cannot cultivate your lands. The water gets contaminated for several kilometres around the nuclear plant. Even if the radiation levels drop after any nuclear disaster, the radioactivity will be invisible. You will only know that it is working on you when you get various forms of cancer, ulcers, and a number of eye and skin diseases. It is a silent killer.'

The group of villagers sitting opposite him was speechless. They were terrified within and petrified outwardly. All of them held their heads still and gave their attention to Prof. Srinivas as he gave that frightening illustration. They did not ask any question immediately, but they all seemed to have a few questions bothering them inside.

The biggest question in each of these thinking heads was, *Will I be alive in such a disaster?*

After a long pause, they all unknowingly asked the same question in unison. 'Can't we stop building the nuclear plant?'

This was the same reaction that the team had in all the villages that they visited so far. The villagers were shell shocked to hear some of the hard facts of nuclear disasters. And they all began to think in the same direction that Aditya had dreamt about.

The mastermind behind this, Aditya, was away from all this – all alone, taking leisurely walk in Indiranagar BDA park in Bengaluru, picking up a few pebbles from the walkway and high-fiving them in air. Kicking a football, which had come on to the walkway, back to the playing children, Aditya jumped in joy when the ball hit the goal post.

'Goal!' cried a few kids.

Aditya chose to be invisible to thousands of men and women who bought into his ideas of greed and fear. He had made Prof. Srinivas's eyes and ears as his own to understand what was happening in obscure interiors of Andhra Pradesh.

He had been calling Srinivas at the end of each day to get the pulse of the villagers.

That night, Prof. Srinivas's phone began to ring.

'Hello, sir. How was the day?' asked Aditya.

'Good. We had a similar reaction from the villagers, as you would wish, today too. They are thinking on the single point agenda that we have – that is, to stall nuclear plant construction at Silluru.'

'Excellent. When do you think the protests would start?'

'I don't know . . . But they all left thinking very intensely. The fear that we have managed to instil should do the magic. We have to let it play on their minds.'

Aditya paused and thought about it. He was stuck on some of the words that Prof. Srinivas used – 'let it play on their minds . . .'

Why should I leave it to the fate of the villagers' thinking? Is there anything else I can do to instigate anti-nuclear protests? he thought.

A strange glow in his eyes indicated that Aditya had hit upon an idea in a flash.

'Can we fly them?' asked Aditya.

'What?' Prof. Srinivas was really confused.

'I am just thinking aloud. Can we get a group of people to fly to Fukushima and Chernobyl, and arrange visits to the nuclear disaster sites?'

Prof. Srinivas was dumbfounded on Aditya's acumen. Again, he clearly appeared opportunistic, thinking on the flying option and offering something that would work in his favour.

If the villagers were to visit the nuclear disaster sites at Fukushima in Japan, they could see and gather firsthand information on what a fresh crisis entailed the nearby villagers. And a visit to Chernobyl could reveal how the life would shape up over the years in the aftermath of a nuclear disaster.

'Brilliant! You have proved that you are a businessman. Let me talk to Venkateswarlu and confirm if this will work,' said Prof. Srinivas.

'It will work. A sponsored trip to Ukraine and Japan,' said Aditya chuckling. 'Let the source of the funds be confidential. Venkateswarlu should feel a genuine concern for the villagers and not our business behind it!'

'Sure. Your identity is anyway unknown in this whole operation.'

CHAPTER 21
HAWKS OVER THE DEAD BODY

Singhania could not believe Vivek's claim that despite his best efforts, sales had reduced. In fact, Vivek and his team had managed to sell zero apartments in the previous month. Sensing an emergency and wanting to take control of things before they completely slipped away, Singhania decided to make a surprise visit to Bengaluru.

En route from the airport, Singhania flipped through a newspaper inside a taxi as a popular item song, *Munni badnam hui, darling tere liye* played in a soft volume.

Cutting the song through the last line, the radio blared, '94.3. Radiooooo One!' What followed had caught his attention.

'The offer to own a dream home cannot get any better,' cried out a male voice. Singhania instantly recognised that it was the same ad that he had approved to be placed on the radio. Picking up the remote control and turning up the volume, Singhania keenly heard the next bit.

'Singhania Realty brings an unbelievable offer. Pay 20 per cent now to own a home in the property of your choice. Absolutely no more payments until you occupy your dream home. Rush, rush, rush! Call 2929 2929. Conditions apply.'

Singhania was happy to hear it. Turning down the volume again, he curiously looked at the driver from behind. There was no reaction in him. The driver was probably trained not to speak to his clients until asked to.

Singhania wanted to ask how the driver felt about the ad but was a little hesitant as something within him told him that the driver would be too low profile for his kind of apartments. But Singhania was still curious.

'What do you think about the ad?' asked Singhania finally to feel the pulse of the common man.

'Sorry, saar?'

'You heard the Singhania Realty ad, no? What do you think about it?'

'What's there to think saar? Whether we pay 20 per cent or 50 per cent now, we need to pay the rest at some time. But who can afford flats at these prices, saar?'

Singhania was dumbfounded on the sensibility of the common man. He recollected the number of iterations that the team had taken over several brainstorming sessions and intense financial projections using Excel sheets to come up with an offer like that. And the common man brushed it off like a piece of scum.

'Are the flats too expensive in Bengaluru?' asked Singhania as if he was an outsider.

'Too expensive, saar!' said the driver.

'But I heard about some price correction.'

'My brother's son works in a software company, saar. Earns five lakhs a year and he wants a home. He told me once that the prices have corrected some 10 per cent. But he said that he has been waiting for some 40 per cent correction.'

'40 per cent correction?' said Singhania, chuckling sarcastically. 'Impossible.'

Singhania resume reading the newspaper.

Vivek was shocked to see Singhania who walked with a straight face into his office.

Am I getting fired? thought Vivek for a second, holding his breath in tension.

'Good morning, sir.'

'May I get a glimpse of the war-footing operations that you claim to have been undertaking for the last one month?' asked Singhania sarcastically.

Breathing out easy, Vivek reached out to Singhania. It was clear that this surprise visit from Singhania had an agenda to cover.

'Sure, sir. Please follow me,' said Vivek.

Singhania was taken to the large office area where the brigade of dozen young girls had been punching and calling the telephone numbers through their systems.

As Singhania stepped into the room, he put his index finger on his mouth, gesturing that it was not necessary to make any announcement. He preferred to watch the telecallers from a distance from behind.

'Sir, this is Priya calling from Singhania Realty . . . ,' sweetly whispered a young girl into the microphone.

There was some delay before the girl said anything again. After close to forty seconds, she said, 'Madam, this is Priya calling from Singhania Realty . . .'

Again some delay. Now after some thirty-five seconds, she again said, 'Sir, this is Priya calling from Singhania Realty . . .'

Breaking into a big frown on his face and looking back at Vivek, Singhania tried to decipher what was happening. But he soon realised that the users at the other end of the line were simply hanging up.

'What the hell!' he whispered to himself. He then walked to another girl who sat two seats away.

'Sir, this is Kavita calling from Singhania Realty . . . ,' she said. Same fate for this caller too.

'Madam, this is Kavita calling form Singhania Realty . . .' This was the fifth call that Singhania followed from this young girl.

The frown on his face had now got bigger. He was stumped, puzzled, and baffled.

He particularly noticed that none of the callers had dropped the style-quotient in their voices. They were not taken aback. They were not disappointed. Just as birds pick up the falling twigs, again and again, and religiously use them in building a nest, the young girls picked up the next number and placed their calls through the system with the same enthusiasm on each of the calls.

Singhania then silently watched the girls call more numbers from the system. For the next thirty minutes, to be precise, he watched a horror show. In those thirty minutes, he had watched them call about 400 people. And not even a single prospect had cared to hear the young girls completely.

Singhania began to wonder, *Why are the users not even giving a chance to make an offer?*

And then something prompted him to doubt Vivek's efforts there.

Turning to Vivek, he asked, 'Where did you get the prospects' list from?'

'Sir, our guys have managed to get a list of Airtel post-paid subscribers. We have applied a set of filters on the data. We selected only those subscribers who are aged above twenty-eight and with a history of spending more than thousand rupees a month,' responded Vivek confidently.

The data at least now sounded credible. Airtel was the largest telecom service provider in Bengaluru, and post-paid users above twenty-eight with good spending record certainly indicated a good list of prospects.

As Singhania tried to digest this, Vivek added, 'In addition to this non-stop 10 a.m. to 5 p.m. telecalling, we rolled out ads on Radio One, Fever 104, and *Bengaluru Times*. All of them focused on our planned message – Pay 20 per cent now and the rest at the time of occupation.'

'No response from that either?' said Singhania, recollecting what he had heard on the radio just a while ago.

Drawing the edges of his lips towards his chin and making a sad face, Vivek silently shook his head thrice from left to right.

'May I see the progress at the township project?' asked Singhania.

Vivek sensed that he was not going to leave him that day without investigating him thoroughly.

'Sure, sir. Let's go.'

Singhania and Vivek reached the township project near BEL circle on the Outer Ring Road.

Standing at almost the centre of the entire project, Singhania could not trace the barbed wire around the site. It seemed very far – 85 acres was certainly a big piece of land.

A park with a fountain was to come up where Singhania and Vivek were then standing at.

Singhania found the land excavated in multiple places, where the residential towers would be built. The foundation work was now completed, and numerous 3" diametric steel bars that made the core of pillars had begun to shoot up into the sky. The pillars up to the first-floor level had already been completed on five of the residential towers on one side. On the other side, only excavation was completed, with the foundation work still waiting to be initiated.

Singhania also found numerous labourers who worked religiously with their yellow safety helmets on.

He closed his eyes for a moment and began to listen to the sounds that filled the air. He heard the machinery at work: concrete mixers, noisy engines of the tippers that dumped sand, occasional shouts from the labourers, and buzzing earth-movers all around.

This is the buzz that a good project should have. And we have it here, he thought to himself.

He then opened his eyes to observe who was coming in.

For the next forty-five minutes, he observed but recognised the emptiness that filled acres and acres of the project. The only men who walked inside the premises were all his men – not even a single prospective customer.

Still in disbelief, he asked after a long time, 'Can you please take me to the Koramangala project?'

Koramangala project was built on 6 acres – a tiny piece of land compared with the 85-acres township project.

Arriving there, Singhania found that the planned eight residential towers were structurally completed. As the flooring work was almost completed, there was hardly any productive buzz – neither his men were at sight nor the machinery. Dotted with a few men who were seen walking up and down the stairs, carrying some electrical cables and plumbing material in their hands, the site was almost deserted.

The quietness of empty business filled the air.

Singhania found, on the contrary, that the streets across the project were gleefully busy. Honking all the way, cars zipped past, and customers hung around in the opened retail outlets.

'What's the unsold inventory of flats here?' asked Singhania.

'Sir, we still have 528 flats.'

'And how many flats do we have here completely?'

'660, sir.'

'How are you comfortably sitting on top of almost 80 per cent unsold inventory?'

Vivek drew his head towards his chest in shame. He was helpless and could not explain it any further.

Singhania found Vivek's silence more disturbing than the silence around him.

Singhania and Vivek then visited JP Nagar and Nagarabhavi projects. By that evening it was clear for Singhania that there was only one common thing and it was 'silence'! There was absolutely no business.

This was the silence that bothered him since that morning – an eerie silence which unsettled him. An unnerving silence pumped his heart to a much-faster pace. A spooky silence let his ears constantly hear his own heartbeat! For the first time in his life, he began to feel an enigmatic fear in this silence.

By the break of the dusk, the tall towering structures behind him began to loom blackly in silhouette. The deafening chasm of silence was filled with shrieking cries of something strange right above his head. He curiously looked up into the sky.

Singhania found a large group of eagles circling right above his head – over a dozen of them, some 200 feet above him. As he watched them, the eagles began spreading into bigger circles all over the project area. The shrieks of the hawks began to grow with the growing size of circles that they had made. The amplifying cries completely filled the silence which had haunted him throughout the day. The circling predators seemed happy with their prey – the lifeless towers of the project. He felt as if a dead body was in his vicinity, and this feeling sent a shudder down Singhania's spine.

'There is something distinctly wrong in Bengaluru!' murmured Singhania. 'I got to do something about this!'

Vivek thought that his job would soon be on the chopping block!

CHAPTER 22
THE UPRISING! 25,000 MORE SOLDIERS IN SILLURU

6.30 a.m.

The gatekeeper of Silluru Nuclear Power Plant arrived in his Khaki uniform as per his daily schedule. This fifty-five-year-old man was always the first person to come to this power plant that was under construction for several months now.

Parking his bicycle inside the premises and walking back slowly towards a table near the main gate, he pulled out a set of four registers. Any incoming person had to sign in one of them. These were separate registers for contract workers, permanent employees, senior managers, and visitors.

Dusting the large wooden table at the main gate, he then neatly placed the registers on it – one beside the other. Taking his seat and pulling out a local newspaper from a cotton bag that was hanging from his shoulders until then, he began reading the headlines.

He read the top headline and some contents below it, and then he heard someone walking towards him – very feebly, though.

Raising and turning his head, he observed who it was. It was too early for any factory worker to come at that hour of the day. He still had another hour before the workers would start coming in.

He found a young woman, carrying her two-year-old child in her hips, walking towards him. But then she abruptly stopped there – some hundred feet away. And then she looked straight into his eyes.

The old gatekeeper squinted his eyes as he watched her curiously for a few seconds. She did nothing but sit on the ground, resting her child in her lap and pushing a milk bottle in the child's mouth.

Indifferent to what he had seen, the old man resumed reading the newspaper.

Flipping the just-completed first page and spreading the newspaper wide open now, he subconsciously looked at the young woman again. By now, two more women joined her, and he had no clue why they sat there, silently.

Are they contract workers? he thought.

He was unable to read the next two headlines, and some content underneath them, properly because the early morning silence and the occasional chirping of birds on that summer morning was intermittently disturbed with unfamiliar noises.

He then raised his head, only to see an unusual sight. He watched a group of five men, arriving from the left-hand side road. He also watched another group of seven men, arriving from the road that was bang opposite the main gate and yet another group of ten men and women, arriving from the right-hand side road.

Who are all these people? he wondered once again.

Not even a single face was familiar to him. They were certainly not from his village.

Noticing that all these men and women silently joined an already growing number of seated people, he doubted if these guys were contract labourers to be added from that day. But he had no information on anyone expected that day.

Each time he had tried rolling his eyes back on to the newspaper, he noticed more men and women arriving from all the roads.

7 a.m.

The old man had not seen a sight like that.

Standing up now, he finally chose to close the newspaper, throwing it aside to comprehend what was happening.

What began with a few people, kicking in a faint cloud of dust as they walked confidently towards the gate, had become a giant storm. It was a tsunami – a tsunami of people. He found that the number of men and women walking towards the power plant multiplied by every second. It was in 'single digits' about twenty minutes ago, in 'tens' ten minutes ago, and now in 'hundreds'. Hundreds of them, briskly walking, from all directions joined the waiting crowd.

He was now very sure that this power plant had no requirement for hundreds of new contract workers.

Walking slowly towards them, he noticed that the crowd had already swollen to an army of thousand men and women!

'Who are you? What did you come here for?' he asked.

'We want to close this power plant!'

When a thousand voices intoned together and shouted back, something that he had not expected, his heart sank into his stomach and skipped a beat or two.

'What?'

The old man sensed that he was in trouble. At the age of fifty-five and with a thousand-member strong army right in front of him, he could possibly not do anything silly.

Turning back, he briskly limped towards the main gate.

Lifting the receiver of a dial phone at the gate and looking frightened towards the crowd, he spoke to somebody on the other end. As he spoke, an already-frightened old man, he dabbed a handkerchief on his profusely sweating forehead.

The old man then disappeared into the premises inside.

7.30 a.m.

Parking his car some two kilometres away from the factory, wading through unfamiliar men and women who had blocked his way, the managing director of the company had finally managed to arrive at the main gate. There he found hundreds of his workers waiting outside the main gate.

Turning towards the crowd, he asked, 'What you want?'

'Shut down this power plant!' about twenty-five people around him said in unison. Hearing that, others soon joined.

'Shut down this power plant!' Now hundred people shouted back. Like an echo amongst mountains, the thundering roar of the people went away from him in each wave of fresh people joining the clamour.

'Shut down, shut down!' This high-decibel voice of the crowd multiplied from a few dozen to hundreds and then thousands who simultaneously said, 'Shut down, shut down!'

The sea of villagers who had managed to gather that day could easily be around 25,000!

The power in their voices, by the time it reached the other end of the sea of people in front of him, had the earth underneath tremble in fear.

Even before he could sense what this was all about, he could see hundreds of placards suddenly showing up over their heads.

There were women with babies that seemed months-old and several other women with toddlers, there were men dressed in *dhoti* and *kurtas*, and there were men in regular pants and shirts; there were old men who had come with their walking sticks, and there were men in their youth, flaunting strong muscles. It seemed that the entire population in all villages near Silluru was there, abandoning all other works that they had and bringing together every one in every home – from toddlers to the old people.

Thousands of the placards that they carried had the disaster pictures from the Fukushima power plant in Japan and the Chernobyl power plant in Ukraine.

The managing director quickly managed to read a few placards: 'Let's stop a disaster like this!', 'We will *not* let this happen in India!', 'It's not a reactor, it's a terminator!', 'We love our farms, homes, and family. We cannot lose them!', and 'You are notorious. You keep us in dark!'

And then there were hundreds more like that.

From the pictures that he could see, the managing director realised what had triggered this protest. But he would not have realised that the villagers were all carrying real, personally clicked photographs on their placards. The photographs had come from a group of fifteen men who travelled to Fukushima and Chernobyl the previous month.

Yes, Aditya had managed to execute this plan.

Through Prof. Srinivas, he had Venkateswarlu select a team of fifteen villagers – a few from each of the villages around Silluru – and the team was divided into two groups. One group went to Japan and the other to Ukraine.

The team which travelled to Fukushima in Japan had a very tough time in approaching the nuclear disaster site. Pushing them away, the policemen near Fukushima shouted at them, 'Do you want to die? Please do not come here again.'

The team in Japan had personally seen numerous rescue camps – hundreds of them – outside the radius of hundred kilometres around Fukushima. The sight of thousands of Japanese at each of these camps, queuing for a piece of bread and soup, living in tents, and sleeping under the night sky had considerably influenced them. The fear had begun to build within.

The team that had been to Chernobyl had managed to visit the nuclear disaster site. The site, which was deserted over two decades ago, was poorly accessible, though. They had seen numerous abandoned homes and factory buildings, which was now a place for wild trees and tall weeds. The closer that they had managed to reach the actual disaster site, they could only find barren land, tracks, and tracks of them, with absolutely no vegetation. The pine-tree forest near the site was reduced to reddish-brown dust and had earned a name, Red Forest. Life, as it seemed there, did not dare to take its rebirth even after twenty-five years since the disaster had struck. The villagers had the shock of their lives – while the ghost of disaster was diligently encased in a concrete mountain, the uninhabited, barren land at Chernobyl was enigmatically eerie and haunting!

'Shut down, shut down!' The synchronised voice of an army of 25,000 men and women shook the earth underneath, again.

The managing director of the Silluru Nuclear Power Plant now turned towards a group of fifty men who had blocked the main gate. Looking straight into his eyes, they shouted, 'Shut down, shut down!'

The managing director gave up the idea of venturing into the office. The wall of panic-stricken villagers was too hard for him to crack that day.

'Fear' had manifested that day into a powerful, impregnable force. He would not know now, but this was what Aditya had masterminded and envisaged to happen.

Stepping aside silently, the managing director pulled out his mobile phone to place a call. He urgently needed to reach an important person in New Delhi.

CHAPTER 23
MAKE OR BREAK

Tapping the table gently, Sushil Tandon impatiently waited at the Taj Mahal Hotel in the Heritage Wing in Mumbai.

After over a week-long persuasion, he had finally managed to get a business lunch appointment with Pritesh Singhania. It was important to meet him urgently and sort out pressing problems which had been troubling Savita Offshore for quite some time.

Joining Sushil, the managing director of Savita Offshore, at the table, Pritesh said, 'My apologies, Sushil. I think you are waiting for a while now.'

'That's fine.'

Extending his arm for a firm handshake, Pritesh asked, 'How are you doing?'

'Just about OK, sir,' said Sushil. 'You know why I am meeting you today.'

Taking a seat and gesturing his guest to do the same, Pritesh said, 'Yes, I do. Let me be very candid here. I operate in a restrained business environment. I resonate with what has been troubling you.'

Sushil got the hint of who Pritesh was referring to. It was his uncle and the chairman, Gaurav Singhania. But he wondered how long he could wait to sort out these things.

'Pritesh, we have already posted two quarterly losses – back-to-back – and you very well know that. Our investors are hammering our share price like hell, and we are living in constant fear that the margin calls might trigger any time. I am in a tremendous pressure to reduce our debt, use our assets well, and generate more revenue. That is the only way we will survive in the market.'

Pritesh sensed the genuine tone of concern in his voice. Sushil's eyebrows were raised and his eyes popped out a little as he waited for Pritesh to respond.

'Sushil, as I did mention, I empathise with your state of affairs . . .'

Interrupting him, Sushil added, 'Sir, this is not a time to share our emotions for each other. I am about to lose my business. I will be fired from my job if I don't bring this situation under control. You understand that?' He could not make himself clearer.

Shrugging his shoulders subtly, throwing the menu back on to the table, Pritesh looked across on to the other tables. Well, actually, he looked at no particular object but only visualised his uncle, Singhania, who would not let him do his own thing.

The contracted assets from Savita – jack-up rigs and drill ships – were neither fully used nor let go. This had not just pinched Savita Offshore but, eventually, made it bleed. With a shrinking balance sheet and bloating debt, Savita had to pledge over 97 per cent of their shares. As of that day, the share price quoted 92 per cent below the all-time high that they had last seen two years ago.

When Pritesh tried bringing up this topic the last time, Singhania had brushed it off. He had felt that Savita Offshore was only trying to demand more compensation, coinciding with the government's pressure to increase production.

Maybe he was too upset with the CAI Report that day. He may listen to me if I bring it up in one-on-one meeting. He is generally very supportive if I make him feel that he is God, Pritesh thought.

'I will talk to Mr Singhania and see what I can do,' said Pritesh, looking back at him.

'Sir, this has been long overdue. He neither wants me to meet him directly nor provides what I need through you. I am in a spot,' said Sushil, shrugging his shoulders and sharing his discomfort. 'I have become too small for him to meet and work out a mutually beneficial deal!'

Sushil was right. Elevating himself to the position of the chairman, Singhania had begun throwing a lot of weight around him. He adopted a delegated-yet-irritatingly-micro-managed style of management. Pritesh had felt a number of times that his uncle had begun losing contact with the world by keeping too much to himself – mostly in the name of his shrewd, selfish business tactics.

The glue that stuck Singhania Energy and Savita Offshore together was trust. And that trust was fast eroding for Singhania in the market, as Pritesh could sense.

Trying to build some trust, Pritesh said, 'Sushil, please don't be emotional here. I promise that I will come back to you very soon. I will never let you go bankrupt. You are my partner, and you can be rest assured of that. Please give me some time, though.'

'Please see to it that you release the unused assets or increase my retainer. My hands are also tied. Please don't force me to terminate the partnership in an unfriendly fashion. This is precise what I wanted to communicate in this meeting.'

The threat to terminate a long-standing business relationship could not be more open than this. While he had already made a promise to keep, Pritesh was unsure if he could deliver on that. Singhania was the man to be approached – urgently.

CHAPTER 24
FROZEN

The sales manager at Renuka Steels walked briskly out of the MD's room towards Shaji. There was a sense of urgency that Shaji could feel from his gait and a hint of fear in his facial expression.

'Shaji, how much of stock do you have on the TMT bars?' asked the sales manager.

'Sir, some 200 tonnes. Why?'

'There is some emergency from our customer. Singhania Realty has cancelled all the backlog orders. We will not get to ship the finished stock now.'

'My god!'

'Please don't schedule any production runs for Singhania. I have begun talking to a few commercial real estate folks. I just hope that we will cut a deal. Now that we have a ready stock of 200 tonnes, maybe there will be some immediate takers.'

'Sir, just being curious. Why did Singhania Realty cancel the order?'

'They posted a huge loss. I don't think you follow stocks.'

'Me and stocks?' said Shaji, chuckling.

'That's OK. By the way, are you or any of your friends looking towards buying an apartment?'

'No, sir. Why?'

'Singhania Realty would like to focus on selling flats in their ongoing projects. They have a lot of flats available. I can get you a good discount in any of their projects. Maybe 25 per cent discount, if you go through me,' said the sales manager, proudly showing off the power of his connections.

'Oh, good. I will try and spread the word, sir.'

'Sure, let me know,' said the manager as he began to leave. 'And no more production for Singhania Realty, OK? Until I give contrary instructions.'

'Sure, sir.'

Shaji stepped aside to a secure area, away from office folks, and began to dial Aditya's phone number on his mobile. He could not wait any longer to give this good news.

'Yes, Shaji. Long time, no news. How are you doing?' answered Aditya.

'I am doing fine, sir. How are you?'

'Great. Did you see the news of Silluru Nuclear Power Plant protests in the newspapers?'

Shaji could not comprehend why Aditya asked this.

'Yes, I did. It's all over the TV. But what's the connection?'

'My dear friend, that is a part of our war against Singhania,' said Aditya and laughed with pride.

'What?' Shaji was astonished but pleasantly surprised. He could not imagine that a protest of that scale could be orchestrated. And he went bonkers to note that this was orchestrated by his ex-boss. On TV and newspapers, the protests had looked so real and true to the sentiments of people around Silluru.

'This is totally out of the blue,' added Shaji.

'Prof. Srinivas has helped me on this. Without all your support, my fight against Singhania would have been a lonely and difficult task,' said Aditya. 'You have all made this possible!'

Realising how sharply Aditya was focused on grabbing every opportunity and hitting Singhania at where it mattered, Shaji said, 'I am very happy for you, sir. And, by the way, I have something interesting to share about Singhania.'

Recollecting the past important information on how Singhania had lifted the steel stocks from Renuka Steels, Aditya said, 'Wow! You are an incredible guy. Go ahead. What's that?'

'Sir, Singhania Realty has cancelled all the backlog orders. Our production has come to a standstill now.'

'Is it? Why?'

'Apparently, these guys posted a huge loss recently. And our sales manager told me that Singhania Realty would like to focus on selling the nearly completed flats now. He has even asked me if I would be interested to buy an apartment. He said that he can get me or my friends 25 per cent discount at any of their projects.'

Aditya was particularly amused that Singhania had begun offering discounts in desperation.

'Yes, they have posted seventy-five crores of loss last quarter. This is interesting – it looks like they are very desperate to cut costs, wherever possible,' said Aditya. 'But did you say that your production has stopped? Is your job safe?'

'Sir, fortunately, there is very little inventory. The earlier orders from Singhania were so huge that we had to move whatever was manufactured at regular intervals to his projects. I understand that our sales guys would now aim to sell the existing inventory to some commercial real estate people.'

'Fine. That would be a good move,' said Aditya. 'Thanks a ton for this information. Bye.'

'Bye.'

Aditya closed his eyes and imagined what might be happening at Singhania Realty projects. What came to his mind were an image of frozen construction and deserted buildings as if they were haunted and no homebuyer was ready to buy, the appearance of projecting steel bars over unfinished floors as if they were spiked hair of madly angry Singhania, the picture of the growing dullness of unpainted grey structures as if they reflected the long, sad face of Singhania. Aditya smiled sadistically at those pleasing images which had come to his mind.

'Hi, Kannan,' said Aditya. 'Good time to talk?'

'Yes, please go ahead.'

'Couple of things – one, how is our call option doing on the Singhania Power & Equipment? Two, it seems that Singhania Realty has cancelled their backlog orders with Shaji's company.'

'Great,' said Kannan, and he almost jumped out his seat as he said, 'Is it true?'

'Yes!'

'Wow! It seems that you have got it spot-on with the Facebook idea,' said Kannan. 'I cannot wait to see the stock crash a little more now. By the way, the call option on Singhania Power & Equipment is doing fine. I am on the top of it constantly.'

When Aditya had confirmed news from Prof. Srinivas that the anti-nuclear protests had begun at Silluru Nuclear Power Plant, he initiated another stock-market operation. Using a new strategy this time, Kannan had advised him to write or sell a call option.

A call option in the equity futures market is a low-risk, hedging instrument that an investor could buy in anticipation of increased share price. An investor would pay a premium with an option to sell at a higher premium. In case the stock price falls, the trader would forgo the premium paid, essentially making a loss but limited to the premium paid.

Writing a call option, on the other hand, carries an unlimited risk. The trader gets the premium in advance at the time of writing the option but has to mandatorily square off the position before the expiry. In case there are no major events to push the share price up before expiry, the premium usually decays to near zero. And there lies the safety of writing a call option.

Essentially, Kannan had advised writing a call option, which was equivalent to going short with an advantage of time-decay. Aditya had sold a call option for a premium of 360 rupees with the expiry due in two more months. By selling a hundred lots, which, in turn, had thousands of shares, Aditya had received seventy crores more for a big bet against Singhania Power!

'Should we go short on Singhania Realty again?' asked Aditya, referring to the fresh money that had been minted on Singhania Power.

'No, let's wait.'

⋯⟨◈⟩⋯

Later in the night, after dinner, Meena asked, 'How are things?'

Meena had very little face time with Aditya who was busy shuttling between Bengaluru and Chennai of late. When he had last mentioned about orchestrating the nuclear protests, she could not believe him. While she was happy, she had her own set of fears. The means of achieving his dream was what had troubled her a little. For someone who sincerely believed in God, that fear was probably natural.

'Exciting,' said Aditya in all his happiness. 'Our ammunition to fight Singhania has now bloated to 145 crores! While we got 75 crores by shorting Singhania Realty before, with the help of Kannan, I have sold the shares of Singhania Power and got another 70 crores.'

'Wow! You are on a roll, Adi!' said Meena. 'And what's happening to the Facebook community?'

'Do you want to see?'

Immediately opening his laptop, Aditya logged on to the Facebook page of The Coolest Real Estate Brigade.

The *Likes* on this page was a stunner! 124,890 members had signed up for an irresistible offer of flat 40 per cent discount. He had requested his Facebook community members to sit tight for two years, but he felt that the wait would be too long. He was astounded by his own progress.

'124,890 members. Wow!' said Aditya.

'Wow!' shouted Meena in excitement.

It was yet another top-of-the-world moment for them.

He did not realise what he had sown in Bengaluru homebuyers' mind when he had created the Facebook community. It was a simple thought, a seed of greed, which had grown and multiplied like a virus. When one became two, two into four, and four into eight, it was only a factor of time before the volume swelled to this overwhelming level.

124,890 members was an incredible army that worked in his favour.

'Thank you for adding your bit to the army – our brigade is now 124,890 members strong and is working round-the-clock in Bengaluru. Today, we have all managed to freeze the construction work in many projects. They are frozen to death! And this is our achievement. I have credible information that the developers have cancelled their orders on various raw materials in order to cut costs. Now, they will do what we have been waiting for. I hear that they have begun offering up to 25 per cent discount. Please stay put here for some more time. Please say *no* to anything less than 40 per cent discount that I had promised to provide you all. Soon, and very soon, it is going to happen. I don't think you will have to wait for two complete years! Best wishes, Aditya,' typed Aditya on Facebook Wall and submitted the message.

Instantaneously, he received thousands of *Likes*, as usual.

When Meena watched all this happen in front of her eyes, she could not control her tears of happiness. She hugged Aditya. She could feel how happy he was. As he tightened his grip around her waist, she said, 'I am very happy. Really, really happy tonight!'

CHAPTER 25

THE CONTAGION OF FEAR

The managing director of Silluru Nuclear Power Plant had frantically called the power ministry in New Delhi several times, explaining the emergency. The bureaucrats reacted as if he was on a long-distance call of yesteryears, when hearing a voice itself was a big deal. He was frustrated when the bureaucrats had failed to visualise what an army of 25,000 villagers looked like.

The managing director had said, '25,000.'

'What?'

The managing director wondered whether that punctuation was a surprise or they did not get the number at all.

'25,000,' repeated the managing director futilely.

That day, the anti-nuclear protests were running well into its twenty-fifth day since it had started at Silluru. The villagers did not budge an inch. Not fidgeting an inch but standing straight and strong, they were all together like an impregnable wall.

It was only the night before when the media had taken a serious standing. For the first time, the anti-nuclear protests, which were rallying in a remote village so far, had been covered on the prime time – the nine o' clock news on the NDTV.

'Mr Venkateswarlu, what are your demands from the government of India?' asked the anchor.

'There is no list of demands, Abhijit. There is just one. That is, we want the Silluru Nuclear Power Plant to be shut down – forever. We want the government to be sensitive to people's livelihood in this region. We understand the risks completely – from the very clear and serious health issues to unforeseen circumstances in likely disasters. We cannot let this happen to us or our children.'

'But, Mr Venkateswarlu, don't you think you are making your demand too unreasonable?'

'I am appalled by your insensitivity to this issue, Abhijit,' said Venkateswarlu, who was visibly irritated with the anchor's question. 'There is nothing called unreasonable in life. For media people like you, who might be earning in crores, the demand of poor people might sound unreasonable. But all we have is one home to live and a small farm to make our living. We are absolutely clear on our priorities, and what matters to us is a safe future.'

'No, no, Mr Venkateswarlu, please don't get me wrong. This is not the media's view or my own personal view . . . but it would be a serious challenge for the government in addressing your concerns. Would you agree that conventional power generation has serious issues and nuclear power could solve serious power-deficiency problems?'

'Power generation issues have been perennial in our country,' said Venkateswarlu. 'Inability to address the supply of coal to thermal plants, age-old technology used in coal mining, industrial power thefts – half of which might be happening with the blessings of local ministers in their constituencies, losses in power distribution worth thousands of crores, pathetic and sub-standard quality of power-distribution equipment, corruption at every level – these are real issues for the government to deal with, if it is really determined to resolve the issues. If so many areas of improvement are available within the conventional thermal power, why do we need a dangerous technology like nuclear? Nobody will survive in a likely disaster!'

'Mr Venkateswarlu, you are now making serious allegations when the issue is really . . .'

Interrupting the anchor, Venkateswarlu said, 'Abhijit, pardon me, I am not making any allegations against anyone here. If you dig into your own media archives, you really know what I am referring to. The point really is that the nuclear technology is laced with dangers, and we, a group of villagers around the Silluru Nuclear Power Plant, are concerned. It directly affects our lives, and we cannot let the construction happen.'

This hot debate on prime time was endlessly going on.

Entertaining millions of urban viewers, who are usually the beneficiaries of limited power supply in the country, this prime-time debate on the television also caught the attention of several others. And those several others included curious and concerned people, who lived by other nuclear power plants elsewhere in India.

———◈———

Debojit Sengupta, Gaurav Singhania, and the pilot of a chartered helicopter of Singhania Enterprises had taken their seats. Singhania had obtained a special permission to fly over a few towns of interest. *Interest* would be an understatement; it was actually of a *serious business concern.*

While the anti-nuclear protests at Silluru Nuclear Power plant had entered its forty-second day, the anti-nuclear protests at almost all other ten major nuclear power plants across the country entered their fifth day. What was written off by the ministry initially as an absurd demand had now become a serious national issue. What was initially construed as an insignificant business event had now become a serious business concern for Singhania and a few other large businesses in the country.

What had started like a small fire, burning a few twigs in the wilderness, had now become an uncontrollable wild forest fire!

This was exactly what Aditya had dreamt. He had sown the seeds of fear, and it was as contagious as a wild forest fire. No one would have noticed, but Aditya had kindled the fire at Silluru, and now the fire reached all the nook and corners of the country. It would be near impossible for a fire of this scale to be doused off by anyone.

Starting from Mumbai, Singhania and Debojit began to fly towards the Shindra Nuclear Power Plant in Gujarat.

The Rann of Kutch region that they flew over looked like a desert of white sand, which essentially was salt sediment on marshy land. Sprinkled with a few shrubs here and there, the land beneath also showed off pigmy trees which fought against the high salinity levels in the soil. As the helicopter flew over the nuclear plant, the team found that the desert-like region suddenly transformed like an oasis of people. Dropping some of the flying altitude, from the height of a thousand feet above the ground, this oasis began to look like an ocean! The crowd comprised at least 1,500 villagers who managed to block all entries to the power plant and stalled all works for the last five days.

'Shut down, shut down!' The synchronised voice was feebly audible to that height in flying helicopter.

'How many nuclear reactors are we supposed to deliver here?' asked Singhania.

'Three.'

'And when is this due?'

'In three weeks from now.'

'Oh my god!'

Singhania began to worry.

'Let's move on,' Singhania instructed the pilot.

Turning the chopper around, the pilot started moving it southwards towards Kone in Karnataka.

Reaching Kone Nuclear Power Plant, the sight was similar. Here the crowd measured between 18,000 and 20,000 villagers, and the protest was well into its fifth day. The spread of this massive turnout seemed like a mini Arabian Sea, which flanked the power plant and was visible from the helicopter – just across this huge gathering of villagers.

'Shut down, shut down' The synchronised voice here was a little more powerful than it was at Shindra.

'When are we supposed to deliver the nuclear reactors here?' asked Singhania.

'Sir, we are done with fabrication, and delivery is actually scheduled for the next month. Just before these protests had begun, our team was running the final set of inspections and tests.'

Singhania wondered how long it might take to settle the matter with the protesting villagers. Considering the turnout here and forty-two days of relentless protests at Silluru, it would be completely unpredictable. His biggest worry now was sales realisations. If the nuclear power plants were not in a position to take the delivery of the nuclear reactors, there was no way he would get his money. It would be very important to have some sales coming in this quarter as planned. Or else, Singhania Power & Equipment would be the next big headache for him on the stock markets.

'What are you doing to stop these protests?' asked Singhania.

'Sir?' asked Debojit.

'Yes, you heard me right! Don't you think you should try and stop these protests?'

'Sir, how can I? We are just supplying critical components. It is the government who has to take the lead.'

'The government is comfortable in sitting pretty. Or else, we would not be touring on this forty-second day of protests at Silluru!' said Singhania. 'For all the hard work that we all have put in, can you afford to indefinitely wait for the payments?'

Debojit stayed mum.

'What's your Plan B?' asked Singhania.

Debojit was even more confused now; the question hung over head like a sharpened sword. He wondered whether Singhania was asking him to look out for another job or referring to a genuine Plan B for Singhania Power & Equipment. He just dared to stare back at Singhania's face.

'Debojit, there are a few more private players like us. Did you ever think of collaborating with them, meeting up with the ministry, and discussing our concerns?' asked Singhania. 'Do you realise that we have crores of rupees at stake here?'

'Yes, sir. We will do it.'

Singhania was frustrated that he had to spoon-feed his CEO.

'I have lost the respect for my CEOs,' said Singhania, looking elsewhere, and then instructed the pilot, 'Let's go to Silluru.'

After travelling for more than an hour, Singhania reached Silluru, located adjacent to Bay of Bengal. Here, Singhania got the shock of his life. This densely populated area had produced an army of 25,000 anti-nuclear protesters, the sight of which was terrifying.

'Shut down, shut down!' The howling hurricane of their voice could break the glass of his window if the chopper was lowered a little more.

As the pilot hovered over this power plant, Singhania got a glimpse of an unforgettable sight. It was the sight of fear that the villagers expressed a thousand feet below. It was the sight of fear which Aditya had experienced years ago when Singhania refused to return his property. That fear, which was engineered by Aditya, multiplied manifold to this scale only to haunt Singhania. This sight of fear reflected Singhania's own pounding and frightened heart.

'Shut down, shut down!' sounded to Singhania's ear like echoing *lub-dub, lub-dub* of his heart.

The contagion of fear was let loose – enough to scare the mighty Singhania for the second time in his life!

'Ganesh, can you please come to my office in another two hours? I have something urgent to talk to,' said Singhania to someone whom he called immediately from the helicopter.

Who is this Ganesh? thought Debojit. *Is he a potential CEO candidate that Singhania wants to talk to?*

CHAPTER 26
THE HANDICAP PLAN

Aditya and Pratap sat inside Casa Piccolo, a restaurant located on the CMH Road in Indiranagar. Gently blowing over a spoonful of piping Cream of Tomato, Aditya sipped a little to feel its rich taste. Circling the spoon inside the soup bowl, Pratap, in the meantime, had a bite of garlic bread.

Aditya visited Casa Piccolo after several months to celebrate the big booty that he had made on the stock market. These days, every dine-out was a celebration of his small victories over Singhania and an opportunity to plan for more. That day's meeting over lunch with Pratap was one such opportunity.

Aditya glanced around the restaurant. It appeared same as ever – same old chairs, simple tables, and same layout of seating. On one side was a half-open side wall, looking over the main road. On the other side was the kitchen, from where smiling waiters emerged – it had the same strain of humble beginnings that he had always loved to see. But that day, Aditya wanted to convert it to a war room.

Sipping another spoon of hot Cream of Tomato, Aditya said, 'If Kannan were not there inside the Indian National Bank, this would not have been possible. On a lighter note, I now clearly know when to go short or when it would be safe to sell a call option.' He chuckled.

'He has always been a brilliant guy.'

Kannan was indeed a brilliant guy. His strategies allowed Aditya to make seventy-five crores by going short on Singhania Realty just before their quarterly results. He also made him another seventy crores by selling the call option on Singhania Power.

'Can you imagine turning around twelve crores into 145 crores in such a short time? He is great!' said Aditya, recapping his success.

Meanwhile, the main course had arrived: Puttanesca Pasta for Aditya and Milanese Pasta for Pratap.

'Thank you,' Aditya wished the waiter as he served and left.

Turning to Pratap, he added, 'We should make this bigger. And here is where I see you coming in.'

'Me?' asked Pratap, downing a couple of *paneer* pieces from the Milanese Pasta.

'Yes, you alone can do this.'

Pratap gave a positive smile back.

'Yes,' said Aditya with a big smile. 'Who else can find a good job for people?'

Pratap wondered if Aditya was looking for a job and, therefore, raised an eyebrow.

'No, not for me. I need you to find a good job for Vivek,' said Aditya. 'Vivek Mathur!'

Pratap dropped the fork in his pasta casserole. 'Vivek Mathur?'

'Yes, he must be shitting in his pants as we speak – a huge loss of seventy-five crores in the last quarter and running towards a similar climax this quarter too. Don't you think he will be safe to keep a few options open?'

'Why not?' asked Pratap. 'It is very intuitive that his job is the chopping block.'

Eating a spoonful of Puttanesca Pasta, Aditya asked, 'So do you think we can do it?'

'Of course, yes!' said Pratap. 'This is a great opportunity to add my bit.'

This was exactly how Aditya's strength had been building. With a small stake in the benefits of a fight, every other person joined Aditya's brigade, making it stronger and tougher.

When a lonely fight transforms into a mighty army, the enemy would notice its power one day.

'And please don't forget that poor sales guy, Satish under Vivek and also that Debojit Sengupta!' Aditya added two more names to be decamped from Singhania's men.

'Yes, leave them to me,' said Pratap. 'I will find very good jobs for all of them. Some Mumbai realtors are scouting for a few good people. And they are good enough for the job!' Pratap threw a big smile with a wink.

'Great. The ultimate choke-off begins now,' said Aditya. 'We have only managed to freeze sales in Singhania Realty and stall the production at Singhania Power. Now when people are gone, Singhania will begin feeling handicapped!'

Pratap could feel the intensity in Aditya's dream of taking on Singhania – a kind of guerrilla warfare, which Singhania might be clueless about. Pratap was glad that he would soon contribute his bit in Aditya's grand choking-off of Singhania.

PART V

THE TWIST

CHAPTER 27
30 PER CENT DISCOUNT

This was Vivek's last resort to muster the realty sales in Bengaluru. He had one more month before the quarter closed, and the sales were pathetic – far worse than the previous quarter.

He stared at the planned newspaper advertisement which was a part of an approved advertisement blitz, a high-decibel idea to openly communicate an irresistible offer.

'Grab this FLAT at 30 per cent discount,' the ad headline read in bold red Arial font over a clean white background with an italicised subtitle in smaller font size, reading, 'Before it is too late!'

In good times, pricing and discount information was usually omitted in print communication, but it was reserved for private discussions with interested homebuyers. When sales seemed to have slipped off the cliff and experiencing a free fall, Vivek knew that these were no good times. When prospect after prospect hung up in silence, not listening to the offers, he knew that these were worst times. And worst times demanded bolder moves.

Vivek studied the title, subtitle and bold expression the advertisement carried. He was impressed by how the offer appeared – clean, bold, and bright.

The rest of the advertisement was graphical. Over a gradient of neon-yellow background, it had project pictures of Singhania Realty's Koramangala, Nagarabhavi, JP Nagar, BEL Circle, Sarjapur Road, Old Madras Road, Yeshwantpur, and Mysore Road projects.

Below these pictures was a qualifier, '8 great locations and 1 great discount. Call and book your apartment *now*!'

Vivek looked impressed with the way this ad had come out. With very few words and catchy images, the ad was simple and straightforward.

Vivek stared at the print ad intensely and found an illusionary image – of a wounded soldier who was riddled with bullets and grounded in a battlefield, and staring at death; struggling to stand up on his legs, as if the weight of his fate was heavier than the desire to get up and surprise the enemy with a spray of bullets; behind the soldier's bold face was the lurking fear and a hint of renunciation. Vivek shuddered with a thought if that image was of his own.

Brushing off illusionary images and looking at Satish, Vivek said, 'Yes, this ad should work! Let's send this to Singhania for his approval.'

CHAPTER 28
THE BIG DISCOVERY

F our weeks later . . .
Aditya received a private message on his Facebook account from Jürgen Knopfler from United Petro. Aditya had not heard from him for several months now.

'How are you? I have some news to share. We have made a big crude oil reserve discovery off South Africa. Our estimates put this around ninety billion barrels – enough to last for the next fifty to seventy years. This will become official news in the next three weeks. I am daring to share this big news at the risk of my job. If this can help you come back, whichever way, I will be very happy.'

This must be very big news. Aditya would not know how much was the world crude oil reserve, but he knew that there were very few big discoveries in the recent past. If a reserve could last for the next fifty years, this must be a very big discovery.

Aditya began to think. Sitting with priceless information, which the rest of the world would only know at a later stage, was overwhelming. *But is there something that I can do about it?* he thought.

He instantaneously recollected his high-diametric pipeline business. It could have been a wonderful business to own. His pipelines could have transported thousands of barrels of crude oil from offshore locations to refineries.

With approximately 150 crores in hand, he could consider buying out an existing small company, if not build one from scratch. But the amount looked too small to buy out a company outright.

Lost in the silence of thinking, Aditya was jolted by the ringtone of his mobile.

Picking up the incoming call from Pratap, Aditya said, 'Yes, Pratap. What's up?'

'Great development. I have managed to find jobs for Vivek and Satish. They both would be moving together to a Mumbai-based realtor. Vivek has just confirmed that he placed his papers and so did Satish.'

'Great! Let go without any noise? Singhania must be very frustrated with them.'

'No, apparently, he had a very heated argument. Vivek mentioned that while there were direct references to search for another job earlier, it seems that Singhania had simply flipped his words during the discussion.'

'And then?'

'I understand that Vivek maintained that he had something good to move on.'

'Anyways, this whole thing worked just as we have planned. Thank you. I will now go short on Singhania Realty – again!' Aditya announced his next steps. 'This news could not have come at a better time than today,' he added.

'Why, anything special about today?'

'Yes, very special,' said Aditya. 'Just between us. Jürgen shared important news – it seems that United Petro has discovered a huge crude oil reserve off South African coast. While I was thinking on how to take advantage of this news, you called me with this good news.'

'Wow!' said Pratap. 'What do you have on your mind?'

'I was thinking about the same pipeline business that we had initiated. How sad that we don't have that business today. I would have scaled up that product line. If we make a killing on the market by going short on Singhania Realty, we can hopefully buy out a small pipelines company. But I am just wondering if there are any other ancillary businesses to oil exploration, drilling, and production that we can consider – something that is substantial enough to own and scale up.'

'Hmm. May I suggest a dirty plan?'

'What's that?'

'This is within my realm of things. I can talk to a few people in the oil and gas industry and get you some business ideas.'

'Great. Why are you saying that it is a dirty plan?'

'Dirty because I will discuss and gather these ideas on the pretext of offering them a job in some renowned company,' said Pratap with a chuckle.

Aditya joined him with a loud laughter.

'Goes without saying, you should also talk to Kannan immediately for some ideas,' added Pratap.

'Yes, I will ring him up right now.'

CHAPTER 29
ANOTHER REALTY CRASH

Another day. Another horror show for Singhania.

Singhania Realty share price began to crash again into a bottomless abyss. It was down 42 per cent on flashed CNBC alerts. The alerts read, 'CNBC Exclusive: Vivek Mathur, CEO, Singhania Realty, resigns – reliable sources.', 'No confirmatory response to CNBC emails and SMS', 'Differences over tumbling realty sales in Bengaluru is the trigger – reliable sources.', 'Analysts expect another bad quarterly results.'

Watching the flashing news on TV, Singhania wished the ticker stopped showing these alerts. The share price slipped by 46 per cent!

Singhania threw his drinking glass and watched it broken against the wall. There was nobody worthwhile in his realty business now to call and blast. He had to let go his frustration somehow. He flung another glass towards the wall.

Singhania noticed his mobile ringing. It was the managing director of Indian National Bank. Singhania knew what this call was for!

Aditya was on a hotline with Kannan.

'Should I square off?' asked Aditya. 'We have made a killing. Our bet made with 120 crores yesterday can now fetch us 750 crores.'

'No, just hang on. I get to hear that our bank has started selling just now. This is an unexpected development, and

Singhania has no funds to avert margin call, which has got triggered now.'

'Wow!'

'Wait for another 8-10 per cent correction and then square off,' instructed Kannan. 'No no, let's be safe. Another 5 per cent off, and you just square off. Bye,' added Kannan as an afterthought.

———❖———

The next day, Pratap called Aditya.

'Here are some business ideas that you can consider – I had one guy who was so passionate about "drilling fluids business". He says additives like specialty lubricants, stuck breakers, loss circulation material, dispersants would be of his choice. Niche, boring business that no one else would like to really talk about,' said Pratap.

'Drilling fluids? Sounds good, huh?'

'Yes, he talked extensively about shale gas exploration and the attractiveness of drilling fluids and allied chemicals. Then there was another guy like you. He preferred a pipelines business.'

'Fine.'

'Quite a few wanted to start a consulting business. Apparently, there is always pots of gold waiting for consultants who bring in technical expertise and advise on improving production, deploying better technology, and bringing know-how of geological rock-setting in various part of the world.'

'Wow! This sounds great but beyond our expertise. Anything else?'

'Yes, couple of these guys mentioned about survey services, survey vessels, jack-up rigs, and drill ships. I could only gather that these are indispensable tools and services.'

'Great. These are very good inputs to consider beyond the pipelines business that we already know. I will mull over these ideas. We have got the dough ready for the party,' said Aditya and laughed happily.

'Is it? How much?'

'Eight hundred crores!'

'Amazing multiplication in just one day. How did you do it?'

'Not me. It's our Kannan – the financial wizard!'

Both shared a hearty laughter.

'Nice way to close the week and celebrate the weekend,' said Pratap.

That Friday night, Aditya spent a lot of time researching on business ideas provided by Pratap. He specifically looked at some of the major Indian players in each of those business areas, business size of the leaders in these segments, total number of players offering similar products or services in the market, and if any of those Indian players were listed on the stock market.

CHAPTER 30
THE GAME OF DECEPTION

The next day, Kannan and Aditya sat in Aditya's drawing room. Aditya spread a few printouts from his research findings and evaluation a few business ideas. He had chanced upon something the night before that indicated that the war against Singhania was not over yet.

'Kannan, look at this space of jack-up rigs and drill ships. There are very few players, not just in India but all over the world. In fact, I could only find three Indian companies listed on the stock markets, and the largest Indian player is ranked in the world's top fifteen.'

Looking at the printout with the company profiles of the three listed players, Kannan nodded in agreement.

Adding to his observations, Aditya said, 'The largest rigs provider, Prakash Drilling Equipment, caters to the public sector oil and gas companies. This smaller player, Savita Offshore, to my understanding, is deriving most of its business from only one client. And that one is Singhania Energy!'

Kannan looked back at Aditya, only to notice a spark in his eyes.

'Yes, this is our opportunity to choke off Singhania,' said Aditya. 'So far, we have managed to trouble him only indirectly. Now is the chance to take the fight head-on. Jürgen is on our side – they have one of the biggest oil discoveries, providing us an opportunity to divert the rigs from Singhania to Jürgen.'

'That's good. But we should gain better understanding of the contractual agreements between Savita Offshore and Singhania Energy before we take a decision – what penalties will we invite by terminating the contracts and so on. I can check with some of our equity analysts at Indian National Bank.' Kannan dropped a cautionary note for Aditya to digest.

'Hmm . . . good point.'

'But yes, I am with you. This is the noose that we can choke off Singhania with. No second thoughts,' said Kannan. 'By the way, how much did Savita make last year?'

'Four hundred and fifty crores. The last two years has been on a declining trend.'

Making a quick inference, Kannan said, 'In which case, the money that we have will be insufficient to buy a majority stake. But declining sales? Did you find any specific reason?'

'Yes, I did. I find that rigs are paid on a daily rate, which is linked with the crude oil price. With the global slowdown and declining oil prices, the sales have been going down for the last two years.'

At this time, Aditya's mobile began to ring. It was Prof. Srinivas calling him from Chennai.

'Yes, sir. How are you?' asked Aditya with a vibrant and happy voice.

'Sorry, Aditya,' said Srinivas with a feeble voice. 'I had to tell your name.'

Srinivas's voice was not only feeble, but it was also clear that he was reeling under some pain. Aditya sensed that there was some trouble.

'What happened to you?' asked Aditya anxiously.

'There was this guy named Ganesh, who had come this morning. Along with Venkateswarlu and two muscular men,' said Prof. Srinivas, struggling to speak up every word. He struggled to breathe in-between each word he spoke. He added, 'They hit me very badly and wanted to know the source of funding for the anti-nuclear protests. I am sorry, Aditya, I had to tell your name. I was afraid of my life when he brandished a knife and put it to my neck.'

Aditya could only imagine how badly he would have been mauled. He never heard of anyone who gathered word by word to painfully construct sentences.

'I am really sorry,' said Aditya, placing a hand on his forehead. 'I never imagined that I could put you in trouble like this.' Aditya wiped his sweating forehead. The sudden bad news had sent shock waves across his body.

Kannan now stared at an anxious-looking Aditya.

'I will come to Chennai now. I cannot leave you alone,' added Aditya.

'Take no trouble, my friend,' said Srinivas, mustering some strength. 'My sedentary lifestyle could not take two big blows of those hefty men. But I am absolutely fine. There is no danger at all. I feel they had come only to get your name and not to kill me or anything like that. I am only calling to alert you. Be prepared. Anything can happen now.'

'OK,' said Aditya. 'I am very sorry for you. I never thought . . .'

'Please don't be sorry,' said Srinivas. 'You have to be very alert now. Take care. Bye.'

'Bye.'

Pouncing on Aditya anxiously, Kannan asked, 'What happened to Prof. Srinivas?'

<hr>

That night, Kannan called back Aditya.

'Ya, Kannan?'

'Did any Ganesh come? I hope you are safe.'

'No worries. I am fine. Nobody has come.'

'OK. Be alert. Please don't open the door without knowing anyone.'

'Sure.'

'Are you OK to discuss some business now? I have put an equity analyst friend on this task, and he has great insights on our story,' said Kannan.

'No problem, go ahead.'

'It seems Savita has been struggling for some time now. While only 50 per cent of their assets are contracted to Singhania Energy, more than 90 per cent of their assets are locked by Singhania. They apparently receive some monthly or quarterly retainer on unused assets. It seems Savita had to agree to those terms as the global recession has provided them with very few opportunities to deploy the rigs elsewhere.'

'OK?'

'While my friend does not have information on the duration of contracts, he says that the contracts are usually renewed every two to three years in this industry. And here comes an interesting piece of information.'

'Yes, I am all ears for you,' said Aditya, listening curiously.

'Savita has loads of debt, and there is a consortium of banks throwing them a few lifelines here and there. And the Indian National Bank is one of these banks!' said Kannan with excitement.

'So is this a troubled company that is best avoided?'

'You can conclude either way,' said Kannan. 'Because they had no other global oil producer to contract their fleet, they have been making lesser revenues. Because they were making lesser revenues with a huge debt, they were posting quarterly losses. But by bringing Jürgen into the picture, our problem is solved!'

'Half-solved, I would say,' said Aditya. 'What about the existing debt burden? Will it not kill us eventually?'

'My friend, Aditya, there is hardly any listed company in India that went bankrupt just because of debt!' Kannan made a grand inference that was worth making a note.

'Give me a break, Kannan. Are you saying that there are no debt-riddled, sick companies on the bourses?'

'I am only saying that they did not go bankrupt only because of debt. There could have been other reasons too.'

'I don't think I get you.'

Caring to explain a little more, Kannan said, 'Debt is just one part of a bad story. If the business is challenged with other fundamental reasons, with diminishing opportunities to make revenues, the business is bound to go bankrupt one day. But if debt is the only problem, the company will not be allowed to go bankrupt. Now listen to this carefully. There is something called corporate debt-restructuring! With this exercise, banks postpone the debt servicing from near term to longer term. There are other options like converting debt into equity. At worse, there could also be some write-offs as bad debts by banks.'

'Wow!' exclaimed Aditya. 'Great insights. What is your final inference on Savita Offshore then?'

'Let's buy them,' said Kannan. 'But we will fall short of some cash. Here is my plan – the game of deception!'

'What? The game of deception?' asked Aditya.

'Yes, Singhania would have known your name or will know it shortly. That mysterious Ganesh would have leaked the information by now. Now imagine this – what if he also comes to know that you are buying Prakash Drilling Equipment?'

'But why Prakash Drilling?'

'Because they are the biggest in the industry. Your thoughts, as manifested in the Bengaluru Real Estate buyers or in that tsunami of people protesting against nuclear establishments are no smaller ideas,' inferred Kannan. 'And by buying Prakash Drilling, we will confuse Singhania on our next moves. And to just stop you from advancing, I feel he will buy us out. We would have made our booty by then!'

Ganesh, understandably Singhania's man, already had his name. He would certainly reveal him as the mastermind behind the realty slowdown and anti-nuclear protests. Aditya imagined how Singhania would react to the likely news of his buying Prakash Drilling amidst such a revelation.

'Incredible idea! I am game for it.'

That night, Aditya received an SMS from Pratap at about 11.50 p.m.

'Hot news: Debojit Sengupta resigned from Singhania Power & Equipment ☺ Singhania is now completely crippled, as you wished! – Pratap.'

'Thank you. You are god! ☺ My wish has been granted so soon,' he replied.

CHAPTER 31
ADITYA KULKARNI UNVEILED

Singhania sat in his presidential office room, with both his hands over his head, perplexed in front of a dossier titled, 'Aditya Kulkarni'.

He was perplexed, confused, and shocked.

'Aditya Kulkarni?' asked Singhania to himself, pulling his hair.

It was a little less than two years ago that Aditya Kulkarni was here in the same office. He still could vividly recollect. He had come and pleaded for his property. He had looked sympathetic, carrying a frail structure and hardly an attention-grabbing body language. He was shooed away with a petty sum that he could afford to throw away.

'That Aditya Kulkarni did this?' Singhania was really mad at the report in front of him.

Ganesh and his team of corporate sleuths had traced the falling Bengaluru realty sales to The Coolest Real Estate Brigade that Aditya Kulkarni had established. And the records showed that he started that community within a month after he was shown the door in this very room!

It was unbelievable how one man's thought could inspire 140,000 homebuyers to postpone their home purchase by two years.

'1,40,000 homebuyers!' exclaimed Singhania in disbelief. That was the latest number of members as of the previous night.

Singhania narrowed his eyes in fierce concentration as he browsed through some of the excerpts of the discussions running on this Facebook community; he was shocked.

The 40 per cent discount offer brought an obscure picture from his memory on to the forefront. Yes, it was the image of the taxi driver who vividly told him that his brother's son, a software employee, was waiting for some 40 per cent correction!

How close I was to the truth that day and how far Aditya has travelled by now, Singhania thought.

Singhania instantaneously recollected his trips to Bengaluru, his realty project site visits, and the war room with a dozen, non-stop callers who worked like soldiers, firing futile bullets.

Here, in front of him, Singhania could see how Aditya had managed to counter his every move, his every attempt to generate some business.

Singhania could never imagine that there was another person on the other side of the fence shooting down every bullet he had fired. He could only see now, but there was one man constantly breathing down his neck, knowing his every move, replicating himself in an unseen army of 1,40,000 homebuyers within Bengaluru and bringing down his realty business!

'A hell of a guy!'

Ganesh and his team also had managed to trace the pathetic performance of Singhania Realty share price to Aditya Kulkarni.

Not only had he invisibly directed and composed the script, but the reports indicated that he had also taken financial advantage of it. He was one of the biggest beneficiaries of falling share price, shorting it with thousands of shares, building weakness in the counter and pushing him into an eventual loss of all the pledged shares!

'Is this the guy who screwed me?' Singhania turned red-faced by now.

For the shock of Singhania, this wasn't the end. There was more that the reports had indicated.

For what he had initially construed as a natural reaction to the Japanese nuclear disaster and later suspected for some invisible hand behind the Indian anti-nuclear protests, this report was shocking. He had never even remotely dreamt that the man who orchestrated them could be Aditya Kulkarni.

It was frightening how that frail, tall young man masterminded a movement that he had witnessed with his own eyes, thousand feet above the protesting villagers, from his own chartered chopper. The contagion of fear that Aditya had managed to spread from just one tiny village to the entire country had now sent another wave of fear to Singhania's head.

Singhania shuddered in fear as if Aditya Kulkarni was a reincarnation of Mahatma Gandhi, another frail but a daring man who had taken the mighty British Empire head-on by doing simple unarguable things and replicated his thoughts in crores of Indians.

It was clear that Aditya Kulkarni was a personification of *Passive Aggression*! *Passive* by the perception anyone builds at first sight, but *aggressive* with the invisible burning desire within. Aditya's name, by now, had suddenly become a monster roar in his ears.

Singhania could see from the report that he not only created those protests, but he had also multiplied his muscle, financially. Singhania could never imagine that he was the seed investor for an enterprise called Aditya Kulkarni. It was as if Singhania was cutting the same branch of the tree on which he sat!

And that enterprise called Aditya Kulkarni had now become even bigger. He would not know it until this moment.

Singhania's mobile began to ring.

'Sir, did it come to your notice that there were several bulk transactions on the Prakash Drilling counter over a last few days?' asked Ganesh.

'No, why?'

'Sir, our guys have managed to trace the transactions to Aditya Kulkarni. We did not cover it in our report submitted to you. But he is right now buying Prakash Drilling Equipment. He has already acquired close to 10 per cent of the company!' said Ganesh.

'OK. Thank you for the information. Bye.'

Throwing his mobile phone at the sofa located in front of the flat-screen TV, Singhania said, 'What on earth is he doing?'

Singhania never dealt with Prakash Drilling. Their fleet was completely tied up with the public sector players. He had only worked with Savita Offshore, the number three in this industry.

Singhania began to think – intensely.

Is he buying Prakash Drilling to launch a fresh attack on me?

Frantically walking up and down his presidential office room for a few more minutes, he asked himself a lot of questions.

Through the Facebook community, he has not only pinched me but also other realty players in Bengaluru. By instigating anti-nuclear protests, he has not only squeezed me but also other power equipment players throughout the country. Why am I feeling that he is only against me?

But then he had other counter, nagging questions.

Why did Aditya short my companies' shares? Then he must be cooking up something only for me! Or did he short the shares of other companies too that Ganesh did not capture? If he has planned an attack against me, why is he buying Prakash Drilling? Why not Savita Offshore?

Singhania had no clarity despite breaking his head for several minutes. And then he decided to do something which could stall Aditya's march ahead – something that Aditya and Kannan had hardly thought about!

Dialling a number on his mobile, Singhania waited for an answer.

'Hello, Mr Singhania, how are you? It's been a long, long time!' said a frail voice with an equally paced fluency of words.

'Yes, Mr Shah, it has been a long time. I am doing fine, and how are you doing, sir?'

Deepak Shah was one of the oldest and biggest investors in the country, and Singhania recollected that he had a huge 24 per cent stake in Prakash Drilling. He would be an important investor to be bought out, if one were to acquire 51 per cent controlling stake.

'Fine, thank you. How can I help you, sir?' asked Shah.

'I heard about this news that someone is aggressively buying Prakash Drilling in the market. Just wanted to know if you sold any of your stake.'

'No, not all. The valuations are too depressed for me to sell out now. I thought someone was doing a smart job of acquiring at these levels. The share price has increased over 78 per cent in the past one week, though.'

'Oh, OK,' said Singhania, losing his concentration to the 78 per cent spike in the stock, a great return that Aditya had already made. But Singhania had an idea that could diminish those returns to nil.

'So I understand that you don't have any plan to sell out,' added Singhania.

'Not for now. But who knows? If the current rate of appreciate continues, even I might be tempted to sell out one day,' said Shah. That was like a bomb being dropped on Singhania's head.

'Why, any problem?' asked Shah as Singhania was silent.

'May I ask you a favour?'

'Sure, go ahead. I can do anything for a good old friend like you,' said Shah.

'I see that the person who is acquiring these shares of Prakash Drilling is an old enemy of mine. Can you please sit tight for me, sir? I don't want him to get to the 51 per cent mark, if at all there was a plan like that!'

'I got it. I will do it for you.'

'Thank you,' said Singhania. 'Thank you so much!'

Singhania was back in the game. And with a bang.

CHAPTER 32
FACING THE WALL, AGAIN

A ditya was facing the wall for the second time in his life.
After relentless buying of Prakash Drilling shares in the market, the number of sellers was fast drying up, and the cost of acquisition was increasing steeply – something that he had not expected.

The share price of Prakash had now reached 175 per cent from his original purchase price, and he was approaching the open offer point. Beyond this, Aditya would get into legal, regulatory tangle to mandatorily offer a price to the rest of the minority stakeholders. And he knew that would come at prohibitively expensive price.

Very frankly, Aditya's war chest was depleting with every acquiring share in the market.

'What's happening?' asked Aditya.

Kannan had no clue where they had gone wrong. His mind stopped working after he began feeling guilty in putting Aditya into this trouble. He kicked himself for changing his plan in buying Savita. The idea of increasing the war chest was not working for now. But he would need to help his friend at any cost.

Opening the shareholder page of Prakash Drilling, Kannan said, 'Please give me a moment.'

Clicking a few buttons and drilling down further in the public shareholders' section, Kannan spent a few minutes trying to understand the data. It took him another minute to figure out how stupid he was in not considering this important data before advising Aditya on this very idea.

It was the data related to the largest individual shareholder in Prakash Drilling – Deepak Shah!

Aditya was also glued on to the screen, and he had his answer to the nagging question troubling him for the past two days.

'Deepak Shah holds 24 per cent of Prakash Drilling?' exclaimed Aditya.

Kannan had no courage to show his face to Aditya now. For ignoring this road-blocking data and pushing him in this direction, Kannan covered his face in shame with both his hands.

'Oh my god! I am extremely sorry, Aditya,' said Kannan, mustering some strength to utter those words. He lowered his right hand and repeatedly hit the table in frustration.

Aditya stayed silent, thinking. He made his decision, and he could not blame anyone else for it. It was his life. It was his war. Fortunately, he had managed to find many soldiers in fighting his cause. And each one of them had helped him in building an army, from strength to strength.

He was the master of his thoughts, words, and deeds. He had to own this piece of failure too.

The war chest of 800 crores, which was painstakingly built so far, would now be near impossible to come back. When he acquired the shares of Prakash Drilling as if there was no one else on this earth, and when he acquired with a speed as if there was no tomorrow, he had to pay the price to buy out the sole, big investor left on this counter.

Slowly, the negative emotions began to bubble up to the surface. Frustration – he had last experienced it when no lawyer was ready to fight in his case. That negative energy began to surge to the surface again.

Fear – he had last experienced it when Singhania was in no mood to return his property two years ago. That terror began to emerge again. Anger – he had it the last time when Singhania orchestrated to cancel the biggest order, called him a beggar, and threw a cheque. He was now angry at himself.

This war against arrogance would be futile to end like this!

He realised that he would need some time to think. He would need some time to control his emotions, apply some thought, and swim to the shore. Or else he would drown in this emotional ocean in no time. His war cannot die this death, for the painstaking effort he and thousands had put in.

'Don't worry. It is not your fault. I have made that decision, and I own this,' said Aditya, placing his hand on Kannan's back and patting him in support.

'We need some time to think and plan our next steps,' added Aditya. Leaving Kannan, Aditya left his office room.

After hours of struggle, Aditya finally managed to find the residential telephone number to call Deepak Shah in Mumbai. He tried reaching him for the rest of the afternoon, but he had no luck. Deepak was out on business, and Aditya was asked to call again later in the evening.

At 8 p.m. that night, speaking into the answered phone, Aditya said, 'May I speak to Mr Shah?'

'Yes, speaking.'

'Sir, I am Aditya Kulkarni calling from Bengaluru.' By then Shah knew who it was. Aditya's name was quoted in most of the business newspapers, and he knew that he was aggressively acquiring the shares of Prakash Drilling.

'Yes, how may I help you?'

Aditya was happy with the polite response.

'Sir, I have been acquiring the shares of Prakash Drilling in the open market. I wish to understand if you would be willing to sell your stake. Only then I can proceed with some more acquisition up to the open offer point.'

'Did you hear that I might be willing to sell out?' asked Shah.

'I am afraid, no.'

'Then?'

Aditya was snubbed. Those seemingly polite words from Shah had punched him in the face. He got his answer.

But then, it suddenly flashed to him: if he was stuck with no more money to acquire any shares, could he not offer his already-acquired shares to Shah? In a flash, he thought he had a great idea.

'May I ask you something, sir?' said Aditya. 'Would you be interested to acquire more shares in Prakash? I am willing to sell out my stake.'

Shah was surprised at this offer and even tempted. But he had made a promise to his friend, Singhania. He had to keep it. He recollected that Singhania had specifically referred Aditya as an old enemy. While Singhania's request was not to sell out his stake, even buying his enemy's stake would also be construed a favour to his enemy.

'No, I have no plans to further increase my stake,' said Shah. 'My apologies.'

There was only one route to exit now. He would have to sell all the acquired stake now in the open market and that would be a difficult proposition. He might not find enough buyers for his stake!

At that moment, his mobile phone began to ring. It was from an unknown number, but from the initial digits of +33, it was clear that the call was from France.

Wondering who could that be, he answered, 'Hello?'

CHAPTER 33
LEGAL ACTION

Singhania sat with his corporate lawyer, lawyer's assistant, and Ganesh along with a dossier titled 'Aditya Kulkarni'.

Singhania initiated his action to intensify to fight against Aditya.

'This is straightforward,' said Singhania. 'It is criminal to instigate anti-nuclear protests against the Indian establishments. The government of India would love us to have identified the criminal behind the uncalled-for movement that held the national interests at ransom.'

'I agree,' said the lawyer.

'Please gather information around his bank transactions to establish the link between the protests and funding,' said Singhania.

'Sure, sir.'

'And what about this?' asked Singhania. 'Masterminding a cartel to work against the business establishments in Bengaluru's realty, putting numerous realtors' business in trouble, and gaining wealth through short-selling shares?'

'Sir, we can indicate masterminding this for personal gain at the cost of business establishments. We can incriminate him for profiteering,' said the lawyer.

Singhania heaved a sigh of relief and felt satisfied. He was determined to bring all his powers together in grounding Aditya.

He had no information on who was behind his business troubles until the other day, but he was clear who it was and why now. He would go to any extent to crush him, again.

Introducing Ganesh to the lawyer and his assistant, Singhania said, 'Please take Ganesh and his team's help, as required.'

'Sure, sir.'

'Sure, sir. I will work with his team,' said Ganesh.

'First, please send an email to Aditya, with the charges levelled on him,' said Singhania. '*Right now!*'

'Sure, sir.'

CHAPTER 34
THE LIFELINE

'Am I speaking to Aaditiya Kulkarni?' asked the caller on the other end. He struggled to pronounce his name.

'Yes? Speaking . . .'

'Hi, I am Patrick,' said the caller. 'Patrick Julian.'

'OK?'

'Is this a good time to discuss with you about Prakash Drilling?'

'Prakash Drilling?' Aditya had no clue on who this Patrick was and what he had to do with the company.

'Yes, I understand that you have accumulated substantial amount of shares in Prakash Drilling,' said Patrick.

'Yes, 22.35 per cent stake as of now.'

'Great,' said Patrick. 'We at Astra Exploration Equipment, in France, have been looking to expand our market.'

Aditya sensed something good.

'OK?'

'Astra Exploration has fifteen jack-up rigs, ten survey vessels, and twenty-three drill ships in our fleet at the moment,' said Patrick. 'And we have been considering South Korean, Chinese, and Indian players for acquisitions. But as you might know, this is a difficult market.'

'That's right,' said Aditya confidently.

'We did talk to Prakash Drilling Equipment in India in the past,' continued Patrick. 'We were told that they are not considering any divestment of majority stake to a foreign partner.'

'OK?'

'May I know if there is any change in that stance?' asked Patrick.

'No, not really,' said Aditya. 'In fact, I was on call with another shareholder, Deepak Shah, to buy out his stake.'

It was true that he was on that call. But the reality was far different from what Aditya was trying to paint here. This sounded like a call with good prospects, and he wanted to fake whatever confidence that he lacked until that moment.

'Deepak Shah, the billionaire investor in India?' asked Patrick.

Aditya noticed that Patrick seemed a well-informed foreign investor.

'Yes,' said Aditya. 'He is not ready to sell his stake for now. I would like to hang on to buy more at a later date.'

'OK,' said Patrick. 'Coming straight to the point. Would you be willing to sell your stake to us? We are willing to acquire your entire stake in one block deal.'

This was the lifeline thrown out of blue. He wanted to jump high in the air and yell, 'Hurray,' but trying to contain the surprise and controlling his excitement and happiness, he silently bite his lips which had begun to part way for a big smile.

He wanted to close the deal – right then.

'Maybe, if there is a deal!' Aditya faked a little diplomacy, controlling his emotions.

'Sure. I will arrange a conference call with my boss, financial department, and other stakeholders in another hour. Would that be fine with you?'

'Absolutely!'

He was amazed that a call from France could pull him out of the trouble.

'Thank you,' added Aditya.

'But I need to thank you and Kannan first,' said Patrick.

'Kannan?'

'Yes, Kannan from the Indian National Bank. He alerted us on this deal,' said Patrick. 'Anyway, I will call you again in an hour. I will now loop in the Indian National Bank to facilitate the discussion. Bye-bye.'

'Bye-bye.'

Now it was clear on the source of this call. His good friend, Kannan, was instrumental in throwing him the lifeline.

Immediately dialling him, Aditya said, 'Hey, Kannan. Thanks a ton. I got this call from Patrick from Astra Exploration.'

'Great!' exclaimed Kannan.

'Thank you so much. I just thought we lost the plot, but we are back!'

Tears of joy gushed out of Aditya's eyes.

Recollecting the prior turmoil, Kannan said, 'My apologies for putting you in that tight spot. I should have thought about it thoroughly. Fortunately, with the help of a good equity analyst here, I was able to reach out to Patrick.'

This is what good friendship would do – connects two people with mutual interests, binds them in trust, and facilitates an enigmatic telepathic communication between them.

'Thank you. You are great, buddy!'

The next day, Aditya noticed an incoming email from Singhania's legal team.

'Mr Kulkarni, this is to incriminate you on two cases. We found you funding and instigating anti-nuclear protests against the Indian national establishments. Any action against national establishments is a culpable crime.

Two, we also have information that you have created a cartel of homebuyers in Bengaluru. You have made personal, financial gains by punting on Singhania Realty shares on the stock markets. You are, again, culpable for this financial crime.'

Aditya was not surprised to see this. If any, he was less surprised. After mauling Prof. Srinivas, he was a little afraid that Singhania might stoop down to the level of a local goon and send his men and harm him and his family. He was glad that he did not do it.

Reading the email again, Aditya gave it a thought for a minute and replied, 'Second thing, first. Please go ahead and frame your charges against me for creating the Facebook community. When the builders can create cartels and sell stuff that is exorbitantly priced for consumers, I too have a reason for my cause. If uniting buyers and merely postponing purchase decisions by two years is crime, so be it. I can fight my case in the court.'

And then he replied to the first charge on anti-nuclear protests that would spin Singhania's head.

CHAPTER 35
SINGHANIA CHOKED!

O ne day later . . .
Singhania impatiently waited for the lawyer, who had apprised him of Aditya's clever email response and was to join him for an urgent discussion in any moment.

Walking up and down the room, Singhania noticed the flash news which appeared on the ticker of the CNBC-TV 18 channel playing in his palatial office.

He could not believe his eyes.

'Block deal on Prakash Drilling: 22.35 per cent stake changed hands in a block deal.' 'Block deal on Prakash Drilling: Deal involved a foreign player.'

'What?' exclaimed Singhania.

Dialling Deepak Shah, Singhania asked, 'Sir, I have come across this flash news on CNBC. There is a block deal on Prakash Drilling.'

'Yes, my friend. I have been informed about it just now.'

'How? Who?'

'No idea. I heard on the market that it is a French player.'

'French player?'

'Let me tell you, Aditya sounded smart to me,' said Shah. 'When I rejected the offer to buy his stake, he immediately twisted the story and asked me if I would like to buy out his stake!'

'Yeah?'

'Yeah. I was tempted,' said Shah. 'But I made a promise to you and so stayed away.'

'OK. Thank you for the information.'

In about five minutes, the lawyer arrived at his office.

'Yes, what's the news from Aditya?' asked Singhania.

'Here it is,' said the lawyer, opening and turning his laptop towards him.

'Second thing, first . . .' began the email, 'and on the first charge: Yes, I did fund the anti-nuclear protests. But please note that the funding has come from Mr Singhania. He funded me for this activity by giving me a cheque of fifteen crores. My discussion with Mr Singhania in Mumbai was specifically with this agenda. Please speak to him before you proceed.'

Singhania received his second jolt for the day!

'What the f@&*!'

What he gave to Aditya that day was not a piece of paper but a piece of rope. And that piece of rope had today turned into his noose!

'Suicidal!' exclaimed Singhania. 'Why did I do it?' He kicked himself.

Pulling his hair in confusion on what to do next, Singhania silently sat there, in the sofa, in front of the big flat-screen TV. Only the volume on the TV was audible for the moment.

'On air is Sushil Tandon,' said the CNBC anchor, 'to update us on the deal that they just closed.'

Singhania turned his head, sat up, and took notice. This was his partner and managing director of Savita Offshore.

'Deal?' murmured Singhania.

'Mr Tandon, can you please take us through the deal?'

'Yes, sure. This is an all-cash deal, which was facilitated by the Indian National Bank,' said Sushil. 'We have decided to offer 51 per cent majority stake to Mr Aditya Kulkarni in an all-cash deal at 15 per cent premium to the current market price. He will take over as the chairman of the company post this deal and subject to shareholder approval.'

Singhania could not believe his eyes and ears.

'What? He has bought the controlling stake of my partner company?' Singhania went mad with the news.

'Sir, will there be any management change in the company?' asked the anchor.

'No. There will be no change,' said Sushil. 'All the senior management team members and I will continue in our functions as usual.'

'Mr Tandon, can you please tell us the implications of this deal on your balance sheet? Will this change the way you service your debt?'

'The finer details of the deal are still work in progress. But by and large, yes, you are right. This all-cash deal is so designed to bring down the debt burden. The finer details can only be shared at a later stage when we have them.'

'Mr Tandon, will there be any other changes that the shareholders might be interested to know?'

'Yes,' said Sushil. 'Going forward, the investing partner would like us to use our assets better. We hope that this will bring in additional revenue for us, particularly helping us in otherwise bleak market conditions. By increasing asset productivity and decreasing debt-burden, we will try and increase our shareholder value.'

'Thank you, Mr Tandon,' said the anchor. 'It is always a pleasure talking to you.'

Singhania switched off the TV and, in frustration, he flung the remote control to shatter against the wall.

While it might look unwarranted, the emotion outburst was hinged on the last sentence that Sushil had made. Singhania was clearly frightened by imminent fall out of events – Sushil might recall all the unused assets, denying him of the tools to produce oil and gas – and its deep business implications for Singhania Energy. This would particularly push him to a corner, even as the government had intensified its pressure for increased production.

Searching for his mobile and putting a number to speed dial, Singhania said, 'Sushil, what have you guys done?'

'I am sorry, Mr Singhania,' said Sushil. 'For months, I chased Pritesh to get an appointment with you to discuss our pain points. You denied that opportunity. When we posted two quarterly losses too, you cared very little in listening to us. We had no option but to take this decision. This is a profitable option for us!'

Sushil could not be more straightforward and blunt.

'So?' shouted back Singhania madly.

'Please prepare for an asset recall. This is one precondition which the new investor is looking for. We are prepared for paying any penalty to cancel all our contracts! I will talk to you later on that,' said Sushil. 'And thank you for remembering and calling me!'

Singhania was speechless. It sounded as if Sushil had slapped him straight.

This is how cash in hand transforms a docile businessman into a more confident, bold, and ruthless one.

At that time, Pritesh Singhania called him.

'Ya, Pritesh?'

'Sir, did you get the news?'

'I have just spoken with Sushil. He has threatened to recall the assets or even cancel all our contracts!'

'No, not that.'

'Then?'

'It is about United Petro's big discovery.'

'What?'

'Yes,' said Pritesh. 'They have discovered ninety billion barrels of oil off the South African coast!'

'What?' exclaimed Singhania.

Putting together the news of big oil discovery and Savita's resolve to recall all their assets, Singhania knew that he was staring into troubled times – he would be screwed big time!

It was clear to him in a flash that Aditya would now divert the rigs to United Petro.

Singhania Energy was his cash-cow business. Without that business, he would have lost his realty business long ago. He ploughed some cash from Singhania Energy for buying all the pledged shares when the margin calls were triggered and was about to lose his business to the bankers.

Singhania was shocked that Aditya had begun to aim at the cash-cow-like energy business. Singhania dreaded in fear when an image of Aditya succeeding one more time popped up in his brain, and at a thought that he would be dragged to the streets.

He had already experience the wrath of the stock market traders on Singhania Realty and Singhania Power & Equipment. He did not want to see the same fate for the Energy business too. He resolved to do something urgently.

PART VI

HAPPILY EVER AFTER

CHAPTER 36
MEETING OF THE TITANS

S inghania sat comfortably on the sofa lying against a window in the modest drawing room of Aditya's residence.

Singhania had to come to Bengaluru. Over several months, his realty business was bleeding, posting two consecutive quarterly losses, taking a severe beating on the stock market, losing senior management team, and depleting thousands of crores from his cash-cow business.

His power equipment business had come to a standstill, denying an opportunity to deliver his products, delaying all incoming payments, forcing him to post huge quarterly losses, losing his chief executive, and witnessing tumbling share prices.

And now, less than a couple of days ago, Aditya had managed to take away his exploration tools, adding to the pressure in increasing the production, putting him in a fix in front the government of India, and potentially escalating the cost of contracting new rigs, which would be very difficult to find.

More than all, Aditya had cleverly tied his hands. He had linked all his allegations back to his own cheque of fifteen crores provided earlier.

He had no other option but to come to Bengaluru. He had to sort this issue out with Aditya that day.

'So what brings you here, Mr Singhania,' said Aditya, 'to this lousy businessman?'

Aditya ensured to take a dig from Singhania's 'lousy businessman' reference that he had made two years earlier.

Giving a glimpse of a frightened smile, Singhania said, 'I see that you have become very smart.'

It was not easy for him to admit that he was wrong in making that inference.

'I thought I would see you much later,' said Aditya, 'when you will be in much more desperate situation.'

'I cannot wait to see my businesses fading into oblivion. I have struggled since my childhood in building my businesses.'

Aditya stared at Singhania for a moment – he did not find a brash corporate giant, but a humbled businessman who recognized where he had come from.

'I am very glad. At least, I have made you recollect your humble beginnings,' said Aditya with no trace of pride or sarcasm. 'Every small entrepreneur will start like you, Mr Singhania. And every small entrepreneur will aspire to grow like you. But, unfortunately, after outgrowing from small beginnings, you have turned arrogant, not minding to crush a small businessman like me. My desires and my beliefs meant nothing to you that day.'

Singhania heard a very different set of words which he had not expected.

Staring at Aditya and introspecting on what he had just said, he stayed silent. It would take some time for him to sink in the spirit of those words.

Maybe he is right, Singhania thought. He recollected his long years of hard work. Along with his hard work came success, and success gave him a lot of power. But he had no clue when his power crisscrossed with arrogance and drove him into hubris.

Realising Singhania was lost into deep thoughts, Aditya asked, 'So how can I help you?'

'I need the access to all the jack-up rigs and drill ships of Savita Offshore. I need you to stop campaigning at your Facebook community, and I need you to stop those anti-nuclear protests.'

The nuclear protests were still going on. That day was the eighty-first day of relentless protests at Silluru; other power plants were also closed for a while. The Facebook community still had investors joining in.

'*Wah*, you still have some courage to come up with these many demands!' said Aditya. 'When I pleaded for my property, the only request that I had that day two years ago, it fell on your deaf ear. And what makes you think that you will get everything that you asked for?'

Word for word. Bullet for bullet. Aditya gave it back to Singhania everything that he had heard from him two years ago.

Confused with what to say next, Singhania went mute for a moment again.

Looking straight at the perplexed Singhania, he added, 'I am sorry, you will not get it until I have something from you. I am sorry, this lousy businessman has turned smart, as you said.'

Realising that this was the moment to find what he could do, Singhania eagerly asked, 'Please tell me what I can do for you.'

'Quite a lot, my friend,' said Aditya. 'I will not forget that you gave me that fifteen crores cheque. It was the oxygen that I needed, even while you choked me off. I am grateful that you provided me that oxygen that day. Or else, I would have died. And probably now is the time I pay you back!'

Singhania was surprised with these words which sounded genuine.

'Remember? I begged and earned my oxygen that day,' said Aditya. 'But you have to pay for it today. Are you ready for that?'

'Yes. Tell me what I need to do,' pleaded Singhania.

'Fine. You need me to give access to the rigs at Savita Offshore, right?'

'Right!'

'You buy me back!' said Aditya.

Singhania was stunned. Aditya had managed to buy 51 per cent stake for almost 1,400 crores.

'Yes, you heard me right. Buy me back. If you need those tools, you are better off owning them forever,' said Aditya. 'Buy me back. My price is 25 per cent more than the price that I have paid.'

'Twenty-five per cent more?'

Leaning over Singhania's face and looking straight into his eyes, Aditya said, 'Yes. My place. My price. Take it or leave it!'

Singhania instantaneously recollected that it was the same phrase that he had used two years ago.

He had no more words to say. He would have to agree if he needed those tools. It would be near impossible to find those many rigs, in a short notice, without making losses for a prolonged time.

Construing Singhania's silence as agreement, Aditya added, 'Then? You need your power equipment business running again, right?'

'Right!'

'Hmm . . . this is difficult,' said Aditya, putting a finger on his mouth and walking in a circle in his room. 'But I have an idea. If you can work together with other players as an industrial consortium, I have an idea.'

'What's that?'

'Can you please put aside some small percentage of your revenues, say something like half a per cent of your sales, into a government-cum-citizen-monitored fund?' asked Aditya. 'This fund is a contingency fund, where together as an industry consortium, you could get financial benefits on the sum – but as long as no nuclear disaster strikes. In case of a disaster, the fund will be used for rehabilitation of people around each of the nuclear plants.'

Aditya then added, 'If you can prepare such a plan, I will work together with NGOs in aligning thousands of villagers to agree to pursue your nuclear power dreams.'

Singhania agreed that this would be a feasible plan, though it might come with a few difficulties in arriving at a consensus, taking a small pinch in revenues. This was certainly not an impossible idea.

'Fine,' said Singhania finally. 'I shall initiate a dialogue with other business owners.'

'Great. And finally, you need me to stop campaigning at my Facebook community, right?'

'Right!'

'Why just stop campaigning? I shall go ahead and give you 1,40,000 customers, if you have so many apartments in Bengaluru to offer!' said Aditya with a roaring and sarcastic laughter.

Returning to his usual self and showing two fingers of his right hand, Aditya added, 'But on two conditions. One, you need to give me back my Whitefield property. Two, you will sell all the apartments that you have at 40 per cent discount to the prices that we had two years ago!'

Singhania was stunned.

'I am sorry,' said Aditya. 'I made two promises that I need to keep – one, to my father that I will take care of his property. Two, to all homebuyers in Bengaluru who signed up with a trust in me that one day I would offer them a property at 40 per cent discount!'

Singhania had a lesson to learn from this no-longer-small-and-lousy businessman.

If one builds an edifice on values, be it a business or any other institution, it will last long. It will certainly see successes coming its way.

He had no option that day but to give in to the demands of Aditya Kulkarni.

'Yes. Done!'

While he had shooed away Aditya that day, treating him like a beggar, today he was invited by Aditya, to his world of new thoughts. Singhania walked out of Aditya's residence with a few things to ponder about.

CHAPTER 37
UNWINDING

Aditya was on the edge of a cliff – seated with his legs hanging down the insurmountable hill. The valley below him and numerous small hills around were full of life – lush green twigs covered up the surface after the recent rains. The green carpet before his eyes, which took the shape along the contours of those hills, was very refreshing. He could stare at it for hours, he thought. From that height, the blue sky appeared to have bowed as if those green hills had a secret to whisper in its ears.

The horizon was the most beautiful thing right in front of his eyes. The clouds looked like large suspended white cotton. At 7,350 feet above sea level, clouds were right on the top of his head. Some of them passed by his side, occasionally, and drizzled all over him. And that early-morning mist was very cool as it hit his face. He drew his denim jacket closer to keep him warm, even as he loved the cool weather.

With folded hands, he eagerly waited for the sun to show up. There were initial indicators of it showing up soon – a red hue appeared in the eastern sky, and chirping birds flew over him, welcoming the daybreak.

After fighting a fierce battle with Singhania, this was a welcome break. Aditya had come with his family to unwind at Ooty – not just Meena, his mother and kids but his entire family: Kannan, Pratap, Prof. Srinivas, Shaji, and all their family members. And then there was a new entrant. It was Sushil Tandon. Aditya had made him resign from Savita Offshore after selling his stake to Singhania. Sushil was hired to head the high-diametric pipeline business. Jürgen had agreed to visit

Bengaluru again in the next few weeks to evaluate and finalise on pipelines to support United Petro's big discovery.

Aditya knew that Ooty was the place to be with his entire family to unwind and make a fresh start again. He had hired a minibus and drove over 290 kilometres from Bengaluru to get to this place.

It was worth the effort – he would get to see beautiful things, like what he was seeing now.

A beautiful, bright-red-coloured sun did show up finally. It got brighter with every passing second, and each one of those seconds provided a different picture of the sun. He did not even wink, intending to enjoy every hue of it.

Aditya had always enjoyed sunrises and sunsets as a child. They had a fascinating short story that could be told within a few minutes – a story that changed each time with a changing backdrop. If it narrated a story with fewer clouds once, it might narrate it differently by placing a silver lining on clouds a few other times. If, sometimes, birds flew towards the sun, they flew away or just passed by a few other times.

Right then the sun was a big, beautiful red ball, and a flock of parrots flew towards the sun, forming a symmetrical 'V' shape. It was amusing to watch birds make such symmetrical shapes. He watched them until they disappeared into the growing brightness of the sun. By now, the sun was super bright to light up all those small hills around. The surrounding hills now flaunted a fresh, sprouting green carpet. It was a rejuvenating moment to watch it live.

Within the next few seconds, a wave of thick cloud came from behind. It was so thick and cool that it sent a chilling sensation down his spine, showering fresh dew all over him. In no time, he got drenched. The cloud was so massive that he could hardly see anything beyond a metre for several minutes.

Eventually, that cloud passed by. The hills looked even more refreshed with that shower of icy-cool dew. The picturesque landscape basking in front of his sparkling eyes brought tears of joy and happiness – something which he did not experience for many years now. He wondered if those moments could last forever.

Wasn't this often called 'heaven'? Wasn't this called happiness?

As tears trickled down his cheeks, he looked up into the sky – a magnificent and vast stretch of blue sky. As he guided his eyes down that way to meet the horizon, he found bluish-grey faraway hills that gleamed in day light. Meanwhile, the numerous hills below him sparkled as they reflected the brightness of the sun in their infinite dewdrops.

It was such a vastness around him that made him insignificant. Probably that was one reason why it inspired countless men on earth to visit mountains. Yes, all for a feeling that man was insignificant before the mammoth structures that God had erected, at time immemorial. And, yes, all for that one feeling that man still had many mysteries to unravel in his life.

On that vast canvas that God painted for the world, he was one dot with God's painting brush.

Aditya found that moment of happiness to flush out all the pride that he had accumulated in winning his war against an otherwise insurmountable corporate gorilla.

Looking back at the journey was amusing. From losing his property to building wealth enough to set up a huge pipelines manufacturing unit, it was worth fighting the war.

'Aditya,' called Meena.

Turning back and rising from his location, Aditya began to walk back. Meena, his mother, and his kids were all together, along with all other family members, waiting to celebrate that morning at a resort in Ooty.

Joining them and approaching Pratap, he said, 'You were right. Everything happens for a good reason.'